WITCH WAY TO MURDER & MAYHEM

THE WITCH WAY MYSTERIES - BOOK 1

JANE HINCHEY

BAYWOLF PRESS · BP · BAYWOLF PRESS

For Alayna, with love from your mom.

AUTHOR'S NOTE

Hey there! Welcome to a whirlwind of whimsy and wonder in my Witch Way Mysteries. If you've got a soft spot for the supernatural, you're in for a real treat.

This is your gateway to a world where magic and mystery intertwine. The Witch Way series has now woven its full tale, but the magic doesn't stop here. For news on my latest adventures and stories, don't forget to sign up for my newsletter.

Janehinchey.com/subscribe

Are you ready to conjure up some fun and unravel a few bewitching puzzles? I'll see you on the other side!

xoxo
Jane

ABOUT THIS BOOK

To call Gran eccentric is somewhat of an understatement. She has questionable fashion sense, cough, can anyone say bedazzled Ugg boots and a tutu? But my Gran? She is awesome. So when she suggested I buy The Dusty Attic Bookstore I was all in, after all, what could go wrong?

Try finding my high school nemesis dead on the floor of my newly acquired store for starters. Now I'm on the suspect list! Okay, so I just need to find the killer, clear my name, and pass my witches exam. Oh, didn't I mention that? Yeah, seems the stunt I pulled on my cheating ex-fiancee cost me not only my job, but my magic.

My name is Harper Jones and this is not how I expected my return to my magical hometown of Whitefall Cove to go.

CHAPTER

ONE

"I'm going to need chicken blood, salt, five candles, and a bottle of vodka."

I looked at Gran in surprise. "Vodka? For the spell?" She was rummaging in the pantry and turned to me triumphantly, a bottle of vodka held aloft. Gran was what everyone called eccentric. She most certainly didn't dress her age, which was eighty, and today's outfit was no exception. Zebra print leggings under a hot pink miniskirt, a leopard print halter top, and Ugg boots.

"No, that's just to celebrate turning his weeny into a teeny tiny pickle."

I laughed, my first true laugh in days. "You know I'm behind you one hundred percent," I said, chuckling and wiping the tears from my eyes, "but one of us with a revoked witch's license is enough, don't you think? Plus, I already put him through hell."

Gran slammed the vodka onto the table, making the vase in the center wobble and the wilting roses drop a few more petals onto the tablecloth. "You were too soft on the cheating weasel," she scolded, placing two shot glasses on the table a little more gently. "A snake? You could have done better."

"Don't forget the monkey. Then a rat," I reminded her. Though I had turned my ex-fiancé into all of those things, I wasn't proud of it. Gran, on the other hand, was indignant I hadn't taken it further—like make Simon's offending appendage drop off.

Simon was an English professor at the East Dondure University in the city. I worked as a librarian for the East Dondure Public Library—that was where we'd met when he came in requesting assistance on a paper he was writing on historical witchcraft from the 1650s. Our shared passion for books and history had been the beginning of a whirlwind courtship, and despite accepting his proposal, a year had passed and we still hadn't set a date. Now there was no need. We'd been at the faculty's annual Christmas Ball when I caught him in the cloak closet with a student. The rage that had roared through me had unleashed my magic in an unholy blast, turning him into creature after creature with no thought or control behind it. Unfortunately, my public display had consequences and here I was, back in Whitefall Cove, living with my gran.

Watching her struggle with the bottle, I took it from her and twisted off the cap, pouring us each a shot.

"Here's to the toad's pecker falling off!" she toasted.

"Gran," I warned, but raised my glass and tossed back the shot, then coughed and gagged, my body protesting as the alcohol burned down my throat and warmed my stomach.

"Lightweight," Gran muttered, not quite under her breath. Another thing about my gran was that she could drink pretty much anyone under the table. Her diminutive size and advanced age were deceptive; she had a cast iron liver and a taste for spirits—not the ghostly kind.

"Child." Reaching across the table, Gran placed her gnarled hand on top of mine and squeezed. "It's good to have you home. I'm sorry it's under such circumstances, but it's still good to have you here. Whitefall Cove has missed you."

"I never thought I'd say this," I admitted, eyes glassy, "but it's good to be back."

I'd been living in the city for five years and hadn't been home in all that time. But after the incident at the Christmas Ball, I'd returned to the apartment I shared with the two-timing rat Simon when the decree from Drixworths Academy of Witchcraft and Wizardry had arrived, suspending my witch's license. Effective immediately. Further instructions to follow. I'd been stunned. I hadn't expected my punishment to be so swift or brutal. Then the text had arrived from my boss. *You're fired.* Perfect, I'd hit the trifecta. I knew then that I was done with city life. My career was over. No one would hire me again, not after the performance they'd all just witnessed, despite being the best librarian the city had ever seen, so I squeezed my belongings into my Lexus and hit the road.

"You're taking all of this very well." Gran peered at me, expression intent, as if she could see into my very soul. Maybe she could?

I shrugged. "Truth be told, Gran, I'm more upset about losing my witch's license than I am about Simon."

"Oh, really?" She perked up at that piece of news. "How so?"

I looked at my left hand where, a week ago, a massive diamond ring had decorated my finger. I'd sold it at a jewelry store on my way out of the city and had pocketed a sweet ten grand. I'd been silently surprised that Simon had bought such an expensive ring, but he was all about appearances. And now that I knew the truth—that his engagement to me was a smokescreen for what he was really up to—I had no qualms about selling it.

I sighed, clenching my fingers and meeting Gran's gaze. "I've done nothing but think about him and that night, and while I'm angry and hurt about the whole thing, I'm not brokenhearted."

"You didn't love him." Gran nodded, and yet I couldn't help but wonder if she really understood. How could she when she'd married the love of her life at eighteen and they'd been together, happy and in love, until the day he died, ten years ago? Although, ever since Pop's passing, Gran had been making up for lost time in the romance stakes.

I blew out a breath, twirling a strand of hair around my finger. "No. I didn't love him." But I'd thought I did. I'd believed myself to be in love with him. I guess he'd done me a favor.

"That's why you wouldn't set a date for the wedding. Despite having that ridiculous bauble on your hand." Gran nodded her head sagely.

"I guess." I hadn't hung around to discuss it with Simon, to ask why he'd cheated on me, or how long it had been going on. I'd been angry, furious even, but buried deep beneath it all was a sense of relief.

"This is where you belong, Harper. Want a waffle?" Gran's ability to jump from one topic to another in the blink of an eye was a skill I'd yet to develop, along with her firecracker attitude to life, and I laughed softly under my breath.

"Sure. Why not?" Ten o'clock at night drinking vodka shots and eating waffles. I'd missed this.

Pulling out her wand, Gran set the kitchen to work and before long, a plate piled high with waffles was sitting in front of us. I missed my magic. My wand was upstairs in my room, as useless to me as a twig. Its magic had been stripped, and I mourned the loss. I'd yet to hear from the Academy about how I could go about restoring my powers, but I held on to the last words of their message—*more instructions to follow.*

"You should buy The Dusty Attic," Gran said, shoveling a mouthful of waffles into her mouth and pointing her fork at me.

"I didn't know it was for sale. What happened to Mr. Dudley?"

"He and Eve retired to Florida six months ago. The bookstore has been sitting empty ever since." She shoveled another mouthful in, nodding. "It would be perfect for you. And prove to the Academy that you're getting some stability in your life."

"Buying a bookstore would prove that?" I said. "Wouldn't they think it was a tad impulsive?"

"Of course not! The Dusty Attic has been waiting for you. It was always meant to be yours."

I choked on a mouthful of waffle, coughing hard, my eyes streaming. When I eventually got myself under control, Gran was still eating, unconcerned.

"What do you mean? About The Dusty Attic being mine?" I wheezed.

She shrugged, waving a hand in the air. "Oh, you know, some things are destined, and this is one of them. We all wondered what that old bookstore was waiting for and when you came home, it hit me. It was waiting for you."

I looked at her, aghast. "How do you know that?"

"I just do. I'm an eighty-year-old witch. I have skills."

She had a point. She'd never steered me wrong. Even when she'd waved goodbye to me when I moved to the city, she'd wished me well and told me that this was just one step on my life's journey and that I would be back in Whitefall Cove one day. I hadn't believed her. I'd set my sights on bigger libraries than what Whitefall Cove could offer, and the East Dondure Public Library had seemed perfect. I made a comfortable salary; I lived in a comfortable apartment, lived a comfortable life. I had everything I thought I ever wanted. And then I didn't.

"I guess it couldn't hurt to take a look."

Stepping into Whitefall Cove's only realtor's office was bittersweet. Seeing my high school nemesis, Whitney Sims, wasn't. Whitney hadn't changed much. Still a tad overweight, still squeezing herself into skin-tight dresses just a smidge too small. Her hair was better. Rather than the blonde frizz she'd battled in high school, she now wore it in long sleek tresses curling over her shoulders, and her makeup was on point. Despite the heavy application, she was actually an attractive woman beneath the war paint.

"Well, well, well, if it isn't Harper Jones. I hear you need my help." Her voice was the same, nails on a blackboard, and a shudder ran up my spine. I plastered a smile on my face.

"It's good to see you again, Whitney," I lied, holding out my hand. She took it, her handshake limp. Wet-fish handshakes made my skin crawl, and I schooled my face to hide my repulsion.

"I hear your career went up in flames." The sneer curling her bright pink lips took me straight back to high school, where she'd taken every opportunity to belittle or antagonize me. I was pleased to say I'd done some growing up since then, but it was apparent Whitney hadn't. She was still the high school bully she'd always been.

"I'm here to sign the papers for The Dusty Attic. You're getting the sale because you're the only realtor in town. Too bad you don't have your own office and have to work out of Palmer Construction," I shot back, taking pleasure in not only standing up for myself, but getting in a shot at Whitney. She wasn't used to me firing back, the flush of color darkening her cheeks testament to her discomfort, but whatever retort she had ready was interrupted by a young, attractive brunette carrying a cardboard tray of takeout coffees.

"Here you go, Whitney," she said with a smile, then looked at me and frowned. "Oh, I'm so sorry. I didn't know Whitney had an appointment this morning or I would have gotten you one, too."

I waved away her apology. "Not a problem. I'm meeting a friend at Bean Me Up after this."

"I'm Christina, by the way." She flashed me a dazzling white smile and set the coffees down on the reception desk, then held out her hand and gave me a firm handshake. I smiled in delight.

"Harper Jones."

"Oh yes, you're buying The Dusty Attic." She nodded enthusiastically. "I'm so excited to see what you'll do with the place."

"Thank you, Christina, that will be all," Whitney cut in, a look of irritation pulling her brows together.

"You'll get lines if you keep frowning like that." The words slipped out before I could stop them and, judging by the stiffening of her spine and the way she squeezed her hand into a fist, Whitney did not appreciate my observation. Again, she was stopped from replying by the door bursting open. This time her husband, Bruce, stepped inside.

He nodded at Christina and then held out a phone to Whitney. "You left this at home."

"Thanks." After taking it from him, she ignored him completely.

He cleared his throat, threw me a smile, and said, "Good to see you, Harper. Your gran sure is happy you're home."

"Oh God," I groaned, "what has she done now?"

He laughed. "Nothing bad, I assure you! Although I'm not sure if you know she's been putting up fliers around town announcing the grand opening of The Dusty Attic?"

"She's what?" I choked, shaking my head. No, I hadn't known. I was signing the final papers this morning and collecting the keys. I was nowhere near ready for a grand opening. But that was typical Gran, ten steps ahead.

"She always was an interfering old biddy," Whitney muttered.

Bruce looked at his wife with an expression I couldn't decipher. I wondered if I had the same look on my face? Whitney really couldn't help herself. "On that note, I've got to run. Once again, welcome home, Harper, and congratulations."

"Thank you."

As he rushed out the door, Mike Palmer, owner of Palmer Construction, came in, talking on his phone.

He paused when he saw me and smiled, lowering the phone for a second.

"Hi, Harper, welcome home." Then his eyes landed on the coffees on the reception desk and he veered over, snatching up the one with his name on the lid. "Thanks, Christina, you're an angel."

"Come on, let's go into my office," Whitney grumbled. "It's a madhouse here this morning."

I waved to Mike and followed Whitney. I'd thought her office would be immaculate, so I was beyond surprised at the chaos that greeted me. Boxes were stacked haphazardly, files were overflowing off the corner of her desk and onto the floor, her bookshelves were an absolute mess and there was clutter everywhere. Back in school, Whitney had been the most organized—the most anal—student of the entire school. What happened?

"Take a seat." She waved to two chairs against the wall, both stacked high with magazines and various papers. I scooped a pile off one chair and gingerly balanced it on top of the pile on the other chair, praying I didn't start a landslide. Dragging the chair up to Whitney's desk, I sat.

She began typing into her computer, ignoring me. I waited her out; knew this was a power play. She hadn't liked me in school and I doubted very much she liked me now. I'd seen her irritation when the others greeted me so warmly. The minutes dragged by and my patience wore thin. Pulling out my phone, I glanced at the time.

"Look, if you're not prepared, we'll have to reschedule," I finally said. "I have another appointment." Although having coffee with Gran wasn't exactly an appointment, I'd promised to meet her and have a celebratory drink at Bean Me Up, the coffee shop directly across the street from my new bookstore.

Her eyes snapped to me. "I'm prepared."

"Well then. What's the hold-up?"

"Listen." Resting her elbows on the desk, she leaned toward me, her face a mask of dislike. "You may be used to the fast-paced city life, but that isn't how things are done here in Whitefall Cove. I'm in charge. I'm the realtor, not you. From what I hear, you got fired as a *librarian*." Her tone told me that my previous occupation was barely above that of a garbage collector in her eyes. I bristled at her insinuation that being a librarian wasn't an honorable or worthy occupation. It was. I loved books; I'd spent hours at Whitefall Cove's only library as a teenager. To lose my job in East Dondure had hurt, but the silver lining was returning home and buying a bookstore. As Gran said, it was meant to be.

Sucking in a deep breath, I closed my eyes and fought for inner calm, before exhaling and opening my eyes to glare at her.

"Like I said, it doesn't look like you're prepared." I stood and prepared to leave. "Call me when you are and I'll come back and sign the papers."

She didn't respond. Instead, she rummaged on her desk, opened a folder and slid a sheaf of papers toward me. "Sign where indicated." She didn't offer a pen, so I dug in my handbag for one, sat back down and obediently signed the papers. A few short minutes later, I was done. The Dusty Attic was mine.

Sliding the contract back across the desk, I waited for Whitney to say something, but when she didn't, I prompted, "Keys?"

She blinked, tugged at the collar of her dress and looked away, unable to meet my eyes.

"Can I deliver them to you later?" she asked, her voice strained, color rising in her cheeks.

She'd lost the keys? Hardly surprising given the state of her office. I opened my mouth, preparing to take my anger out on her, but flashes of Simon and the episode in East Dondure flashed through my mind. *Control, Harper.* Focusing on regulating my breathing and not letting her see how much her incompetence affected me, I gave a brief nod.

"Sure." I stood, slinging my bag over my shoulder. "Let's meet at The Dusty Attic at ten." I'd give her an hour to find the keys.

Nodding curtly, she said, "I'll see you then."

TWO

I'd always suspected Whitney Sims was a Spanks-wearing witch and now I had irrefutable proof. Unfortunately, the fact that Whitney was sprawled unmoving across the floor of my newly purchased bookstore, with the hem of her dress revealing her underwear, took away from my delight at being correct.

"Whitney?" Tossing my bag on the floor by the front door, I hurried across to her and pressed my fingers to her neck, watching for the rise and fall of her chest. Nothing. No pulse. Not breathing. Whitney was no longer in the land of the living. "Great." Sitting back on my haunches, I pulled out my phone and dialed.

"Yes, hello, this is Harper Jones. I'm at The Dusty Attic on Main Street and I'd like to report a death. Yes. It's Whitney Sims. Yes, I'm sure. I've checked her pulse, and she's not breathing. No, I haven't touched anything. I will, thank you." Hanging up, I turned my attention to the body before me.

"So, Whitney, what happened to you, huh?" I wasn't surprised when no answer was forthcoming.

The bell above the door jingled. "Congratulations!" Jenna, my best friend and Fae, bustled inside, arms full of flowers, a bouquet that was a riot of colors and scents. Then she saw Whitney. "Oh."

"Yeah." I nodded solemnly, then stepped forward to take the flowers from Jenna, burying my face in the soft petals. "Thanks for these."

"You're welcome. Ummm. What's Whitney doing on the floor? And is she..." Her voice dropped in that way people had when speaking of the deceased.

"Dead? Yes. I've called the police."

Jenna nodded. "Good. There's still time." Reaching into her purse, she pulled out her phone and began taking pictures. "What happened?"

"Honestly, I don't know. I arranged to meet her here at ten for the handover of the keys. The door was unlocked when I got here, and I found her like this."

"Are you okay?" Jenna paused in her photo-taking frenzy to look my way.

"I'm fine," I reassured her, giving her a weak smile. "It's just that I thought things couldn't get worse, you know?"

"I know, hon. You were so excited about this place.

A fresh start. New beginnings. Don't fret, it can still happen."

"Having Whitney Sims dead in the middle of the floor has kinda taken the shine off," I grumbled. I shivered, rubbing my hands up and down my arms. "It's cold in here, right?" I hadn't noticed immediately, too intent on Whitney to pay any attention to the freezing temperature in the store.

"Let's go find the thermostat. It's probably out the back." Satisfied she'd taken enough photographs, Jenna slid her phone back into her purse and together we searched for the thermostat, eventually finding it in the storeroom out back. I flicked on the heating and listened as it wheezed to life.

"That doesn't sound good," I muttered, making a mental note to get it looked at as soon as possible.

"The Dusty Attic has been closed for months," Jenna said. "It just needs a little TLC is all."

Once upon a time, I would have delivered that TLC with a wave of my wand, but not today. With my magic on lockdown, everything had to be done the old-fashioned way. Manual labor.

The bell above the door jingled again, and we stepped out of the storeroom to see a policewoman enter. She headed straight for Whitney, checked she was dead and then spoke into the radio clipped to her shoulder before turning her attention to us.

"Harper Jones?"

I stepped forward. "Yes."

"Ms. Jones, I'm Police Officer Liliana Miles of the Whitefall Cove Police Department." She tapped the badge pinned to her belt. "Take me through what happened." Pulling out a notebook and pen, she waited, hand poised.

"Well," I began, "I've just bought The Dusty Attic bookstore, and Whitney is the realtor managing the sale. I'd arranged to meet her here this morning at ten for handover of the keys. She must have gotten here before me because the door was unlocked when I got here. I came in and found her like this."

"Have you touched anything?"

"I checked her pulse. Other than opening the front door and turning on the thermostat, I haven't touched a thing."

"And you," Officer Miles turned her attention to Jenna. "What are you doing here?" Before Jenna could answer, she swiveled her gaze back to me. "Did you call the press?"

"No, she didn't," Jenna cut in. "I'm a friend of Harper's. I dropped by to congratulate her and give her these." She pointed to the bouquet I'd laid on the counter. Jenna was a reporter for our local paper, the *Whitefall Cove Tribune*, and was apparently known to Officer Miles.

"Right." She flipped her notebook closed. "I'm

going to have to ask you both to wait outside. But first," she held her hand out to Jenna, "hand it over."

"What?" Jenna played dumb, but Officer Miles wasn't buying it.

"Your phone. I know you've taken photos. Your footprints are all around the body. Now give."

"Fine!" she huffed, slapping her phone into Officer Miles's outstretched hand. I stood silently while the police woman flicked through the images and then diligently deleted each and every one. Jenna rolled her eyes at me and mimed being hung, and I bit back a laugh.

Handing the phone back, Officer Miles pointed to the door. "Wait outside."

"It's freezing out there," I protested, looking out the window at the gray winter day outside.

"It's freezing in here," Officer Miles pointed out, "and until we determine what has happened to Mrs. Sims, this is a crime scene."

"What if we wait at Bean Me Up?" Jenna asked. "Would that be okay?"

"Don't you have to get back to work?" I whispered to Jenna.

She shook her head and whispered back, "Not when my editor hears I'm at the scene of a breaking story. This might get me off obituaries this week."

"Fine." Officer Miles turned her back, and we were dismissed.

Snatching up my bag, I buttoned my coat and followed Jenna outside. I linked her arm with mine and we crossed the street to the coffee shop. It was like stepping into a Christmas wonderland—decorations abounded, and a massive Christmas tree dominated one corner, the star on the top brushing the ceiling. Christmas carols played over the speakers and I felt it from the tips of my toes to the top of my head. I was home.

We snagged a table by the window and ordered hot chocolates while watching the arrival of a paramedic unit, lights flashing but no siren, at The Dusty Attic. Jenna snapped more pictures through the window.

"Thanks for waiting with me," I said, blowing on my drink.

"Oh please, you're giving me the inside scoop on a hot story." Jenna waved her hand over her cup, then did the same to mine, bringing the temperature of the boiling milk down to a drinkable level. I missed my magic. Funny, after everything that had happened, I would have thought I'd miss my fiancé. Or my job. And while those things left a hollow feeling in my chest, I missed my magic the most and that spoke volumes about the life I'd led in the city. Had it been a lie all along? I'd spent the last five years climbing my way up the librarian ladder. I'd just been promoted to head librarian when it all came crashing down, and yet now? I didn't miss it all that much.

"It's good to have you back home. We've missed you." Jenna smiled, and I laughed out loud at the milk mustache she now sported.

"I never thought I'd say this, but I've missed Whitefall Cove too," I admitted, taking a gulp of my drink and showing off my own milk mustache.

And that's the moment a tall, dark, and handsome man came up to our table and said, "Harper Jones?"

I looked up, eyes widening. He was drop-dead gorgeous and my heart did a little flutter. "Yes?" I squeaked.

"Detective Jackson Ward. Mind if I sit down?"

Clearing my throat, I said, "By all means."

He turned away to hook a chair and Jenna madly signaled at me to wipe the milk mustache off my face. I couldn't help it. I laughed. Trust my luck that a handsome detective turned up right when I was looking the fool.

"Something funny?" he asked, and I immediately sobered and shook my head.

"Take me through what happened." Unlike Officer Miles earlier, he didn't take out a notebook and pen, just pinned me with his intense green eyes.

"I already told Officer Miles what happened," I said.

"And now I need you to tell me." His tone indicated

he was in no mood to play games, so I repeated verbatim what I'd told Officer Miles.

"How well did you know Whitney Sims?"

"Pretty well. We went to school together," I answered.

"You were friends?" he pressed.

I snorted. "Hardly. Frenemies is more accurate."

"Frenemies?" A dark brow arched, and he looked at me with his head cocked to one side.

"On the surface, we acted friendly, but the reality was we couldn't stand each other. She was a bully, and I didn't like her. And she didn't like me."

"So, you'd have reason to cause her harm?"

His question shook me to my bones. "No! Of course not," I said. "Whitney and I may not have liked each other, but I didn't wish her harm, and I certainly didn't want her dead. She's only in my store because I'd just purchased it and she was the realtor handling the sale. For the Dudley's." It occurred to me that if he was asking if I had reason to harm Whitney, then he must think her death was suspicious. "Wait. You think foul play? That she was murdered?" My voice dropped on the last word.

"We don't know the cause of death," he replied, not giving an inch. "Until we do, don't leave town."

I snorted. "Hardly. Don't worry, Detective, I'll be around."

"Thank you for your time." He got up and left, giving Jenna a curt nod as he passed.

I waited until he'd left the coffee shop before fanning my face and winking at Jenna. "Phew, that man is—"

She cut me off. "Taken. Detective Jackson Ward is currently dating Police Officer Liliana Miles," she informed me.

"Figures." I sipped my hot chocolate again, watching out the window as Whitney Sims was wheeled out in a black body bag and loaded into the back of a nondescript van that had pulled up behind the medics. "How come you know this?" I murmured.

Jenna chuckled, but didn't lower her phone from capturing the scene outside. "You've forgotten what it's like in a small town, haven't you, Harper? Everyone knows everything about everyone else. Or think they do. And what they don't know, they make up. The handsome detective, for example, arrived in our town two years ago. Single. And despite every eligible female in Whitefall Cove throwing themselves at him, he didn't date. Rumors abounded he was gay. Then Liliana Miles transferred here last year and six months later, they're dating."

I plastered a smile on my face. "Well, good for them."

Jenna glanced at her watch, then gave me an

apologetic smile. "I've gotta get back to the office and write this up. You'll be okay?"

"I'm fine. You still coming over this evening?" We'd arranged to have a mini-celebration at Gran's house. Jenna, myself, and my other best friend Monica.

"Of course. Eight o'clock, right?"

"Yep. I'll see you then." We left together, Jenna hurrying toward the *Tribune's* offices only a few doors down from The Dusty Attic. Shivering, I pulled my coat tighter around myself, glanced once again at the heavy clouds overhead and wondered if we'd get rain. There was something about cozying up inside in front of a fire with a good book on a rainy winter's day—providing you hadn't just found a dead body.

"This is all your fault." Jenna slurred her words, eyeballing Monica, who was acting as hostess and making us the most delicious cocktails.

"I hope so." She grinned, placing a glass in front of me full of rainbow colors that slowly swirled in the glass. Monica was the polar opposite of Jenna. Where Jenna was blonde and small, Monica was dark and tall. The word svelte came to mind. Both were beautiful, but Monica had an otherworldly allure, with her jet-black hair and equally dark eyes, and ruby red lips. Monica was also a vampire.

"Where's mine?" Gran came bustling into the kitchen and my jaw dropped. This evening, she was in a gold sequined mini dress with a plunging neckline. Unfortunately, Gran had plunging breasts to go with the dress, and the overall effect was appalling. She'd thrown an old gray cardigan over the top that was at odds with the glamorous dress, and on her feet, her favorite Ugg boots—she had a friend in Australia who regularly sent her Uggs to add to her collection.

"I've got you covered, Gran." Monica produced a massive cocktail glass filled to the brim. She ushered Gran into a chair and placed the drink in front of her, adding a straw with a flourish. "Enjoy."

"You're my favorite, you know," Gran told her, smiling and wrapping her lips around the straw. Her eyes widened. "Girl! You've got skills," she crowed, smacking her lips in approval and going in for another taste.

I laughed. My good mood from purchasing The Dusty Attic had taken a blow at finding Whitney dead inside, but my two best friends, plus Gran, had pulled me out of the slump, insisting we celebrate anyway. I was glad we had, and I was doubly glad I had such good people around me. Jenna, Monica and I had gone to school together. Monica had been born a vampire, which meant she aged normally as a child, then her aging process slowed down when she hit twenty-five, so despite all of us reaching thirty-two this year,

Monica had aged—or not aged—the best. I'd been gone five years, and yet sitting here tonight, it was as if no time had passed at all.

"Thank you." I smiled at each of them individually, reaching out to clasp their hands across the table. "Thank you so much for this—for being here for me, for being my friends. You mean the world to me."

"Oh God." Gran rolled her eyes and nudged Monica. "She's getting all sentimental. I haven't had enough to drink for that!"

"Gran!" I protested with a laugh. Our frivolity was interrupted by a knocking at the front door.

"Get that, will you, Harper?" Gran ordered. "I'm not leaving this table until I'm done with this drink."

Shaking my head, I made my way down the hallway to the front door, expecting to find one of Gran's friends on the other side. I did not expect Detective Ward.

"Evening." He nodded at me, rubbing his hands together for warmth.

"Detective." I did a poor job at hiding my surprise. "Um, come in. It's cold out."

Closing the front door behind us, I winced at the raucous laughter coming from the kitchen at the back of the house. Instead, I directed him into the living room. Gran had outdone herself with the Christmas decorations in there. Baubles in a riot of colors were suspended from the ceiling, boughs of holly strung across the top of the window, a red Christmas tree stood majestically in the corner with an ever-growing mountain of presents beneath it, and pinned above the door, mistletoe.

I went to light the fire with a snap of my wand, then blushed when nothing happened. I'd forgotten, for a moment, that my magic had been suspended. With a huff, I snatched up the lighter from the mantel and put it to the logs waiting in the fireplace. With a click, the flame took hold.

"You don't have to light that for me," he said.

"Now you tell me," I muttered to myself, but out loud I simply smiled and said, "That's okay, it won't be wasted."

He was watching me intently, making me uncomfortable, so I waved a hand at the sofa. "Please, take a seat. What can I do for you this evening?"

Obviously, he was here about Whitney, but I really wasn't sure what else I could tell him. Which meant there'd been a development. And that development had led him to my door. I was pretty sure it was a development I wasn't going to like and a deep sense of unease set up residence in my bones, making me nervous. I began pacing in front of the fire.

"Ms. Jones. Please. Have a seat."

I twisted my hands together, stopped pacing to look at him, then resumed the back and forth in front of the fireplace, the fire doing little to warm the cold that had settled in my belly. "I don't think I can," I whispered, for a feeling of doom had settled over me, as cold and icy as the weather outside.

"Please?" He breathed the word softly, his voice kinder than before. I cocked my head, then nodded, easing my butt onto the edge of a chair.

"Just tell me," I blurted. Far better to get straight to the point than drag this out and have my imagination conjuring up all sorts of scenarios that probably—hopefully—weren't true.

"Early tests indicate that Whitney Sims did not die a natural death," he said, his eyes not leaving my face.

I swallowed. "She was murdered?" I'd convinced myself that Whitney had suffered a heart attack. The fact that she hadn't was a rude shock.

"Poisoned," he replied.

"Right." I nodded, pushing down the hysteria threatening to consume me. How did my life get so complicated? Until recently, I'd had it all. Now here I was, living with my Gran, unemployed, no magic, and now a suspect in a murder.

"I am a suspect, aren't I?" I asked, just to confirm what I already knew.

"You are a person of interest," he confirmed. "Her body was found in your store."

"One I have only just purchased. Like, literally today. She was meeting me there to hand over the keys. I've told you this."

"We don't think the poison was administered there."

"Oh. Right. Good. But then why am I a suspect?"

"You were with Mrs. Sims earlier, correct?"

"Yes. I was at Palmer Construction offices to sign the papers. But I wasn't the only one there. And I didn't see Whitney eat or drink anything. The receptionist returned with a tray of takeaway coffees —well, I assume they were coffee. They could have been anything really, hot chocolate, tea."

"Ms. Jones," he interrupted, and I blushed again. The alcohol I'd consumed was not helping with keeping my thoughts straight.

"Please call me Harper." Ms. Jones reminded me of the life I'd left behind in the city. The students who'd traipsed in and out of the library had called me Ms. Jones.

Ignoring my request, he continued, "Ms. Jones, can you please take me through, in as much detail as you can, your meeting with Mrs. Sims this morning? No detail is too small or insignificant." He reached into his pocket and pulled out his phone. "Do you mind if I record this?"

I shook my head. Outside, a gust of wind buffeted the window and I shivered again.

"Begin from when you arrived at Palmer Construction," he instructed, hitting record on his phone. Obediently, I relayed what had transpired earlier that day when I'd arrived to sign the papers to purchase The Dusty Attic. After I was done, he thanked me and left. Stunned, I returned to the kitchen to tell the others I was now a suspect in the murder of Whitney Sims.

CHAPTER
THREE

"I had a thought," I said to Gran over breakfast the following morning.

"Oh, no."

"I swear it's a good one this time," I protested.

"Let's hear it." She sipped her coffee and waited.

"I go to Detective Ward and ask to help with the investigation."

"Help how?" Gran asked.

"I'm not sure yet," I admitted, "but it beats sitting around doing nothing. After everything that has happened recently, this is the worst. I'm not a murderer." Although I doubted the detective would be entirely thrilled with the idea of a suspect muscling in on his investigation, I couldn't sit back and do nothing. This was my do-over, my chance at redemption, and Whitney Sims was ruining it. Trust her to die in *my* store.

"I know you're not, dear. You're a librarian." She smiled indulgently.

"Nope." I shook my head. "I'm a bookstore owner. Only I can't even get that right."

"Hey," she leaned forward to take my hand. "None of this is your fault. Don't ever think that. You're right, though. Sitting here stewing over the whole ghastly matter isn't helping. Why not see the detective and find out when you can get access to The Dusty Attic? We have a grand opening to plan."

I studied her through narrowed eyes. "I thought you already put fliers up about that?"

She shrugged a "maybe" before carrying her dishes to the sink, where they promptly began washing themselves. I sat for a moment longer, then decided I'd go see the detective. I had a right to clear my name. And Gran had a point. I needed to know when I could have access to my store.

Pulling on my coat and slinging my bag over my shoulder, I called out goodbye and headed out. First stop, the police station.

Snagging a park right outside the building, I smoothed my palms down my jeans-clad thighs, and approached the door, a fluttering of nerves in my belly. I was right to be nervous. When I stepped inside, all activity stopped and if the silence hadn't been so disconcerting, it would have been hilarious. Heads swiveled to watch my progress as I approached the counter.

"Can I help you?" It was Officer Miles. I gave her a small smile that she didn't return and rested my hands on the counter.

"I was wondering if I could speak with Detective Ward?" I asked.

"You can talk to me," she said. I don't know what it was, but I got the distinct impression she didn't like me, and I wondered what I'd done to deserve it. She was as frosty as a snowman and it showed. I wouldn't have been surprised if her breath had been visible in the air.

"I was really hoping to talk with the detective." I chewed my lip, a little apprehensive of the glare she was giving me. If her demeanor was frosty, her glare was the polar opposite. If she could zap me with her eyeballs, she would. Which begged the question, why? "I would like an update on the case, and I need to know when you'll return the keys to The Dusty Attic— I have a business to run."

Blowing out an irritated sigh, she placed her palms on the counter and leaned forward, jaw tight. "Listen," she began, but was interrupted before she could gather steam by Detective Ward coming around the corner, pulling on his jacket, then pausing when he saw me.

"I was just coming to see you," he said, and I smiled weakly.

"Here I am?" I didn't mean it to sound like a question, but it did. This whole situation was farcical, from Whitney inconveniently dying in my store, to me being a suspect, to Officer Miles appearing to be more than willing to slap me behind bars and throw away the keys, despite me being innocent.

He looked over my head at the officers who'd been watching the whole interaction unfold. "You lot got nothing to do?" he drawled. I heard a bustle of activity behind me and it almost killed me not to turn around and look.

"She was requesting to see you," Officer Miles said, voice icy. "I was just telling her she can speak to me."

"Thanks for the initiative, Liliana, but I've got this. I wanted to talk with Ms. Jones anyway." He turned his attention back to me. "Fancy a coffee?"

"Here?" I could just imagine how that would look. Tongues would wag and the grapevine would have me hung and quartered before I could blink.

"Good grief no. The coffee here is swill. Bean Me Up okay with you?"

I nodded. "Sounds good." Stepping away from the counter, I followed him out the front door.

"Mind if we walk?" he asked once we were outside. The police station was located a couple of blocks over from Main Street. It was a ten-minute walk, tops.

"That's fine." Burying my hands in my pockets, I noted he matched his long stride to my shorter one. Simon had always been two steps ahead whenever we'd been out together.

"You wanted to see me?" I asked.

"Yeah. I've been looking into you—" At my groan, he quickly added, "Purely routine. Anyway, as I was saying, I was looking into your background. I see you were a librarian at East Dondure Library and that you are especially skilled at research? In fact, you helped a lot of the East Dondure University students with their dissertations?"

"That's right." I nodded. "Do you need help with something, Detective?" I was intrigued. While I'd been hopeful of muscling in on his investigation, I hadn't expected him to come to me. Was this too good to be true?

"I do. Did you know that? Is that why you came to the station? You know, your witchy skills in play?"

I shook my head. "I came to the station to see if I could get the keys back to The Dusty Attic. And to see if I could assist in any way because being a suspect in a murder case is not sitting well with me at all. You said you've been looking into me, so you know what happened in East Dondure with my fiancé?"

He nodded. "I do."

"So, you'd know that I not only got fired, but my witch's license has been suspended?"

As we walked, I could feel him looking at me.

"I didn't know about your witch's license. I'm not that familiar with witch law."

"Well, let's just say I broke the cardinal rule of not using magic for harm. The Academy suspended my license—so basically my magic is on lockdown."

"The Academy?"

"Drixworths Academy of Witchcraft and Wizardry," I explained. "Kinda like a witches' council."

"You said 'suspended'. Does that mean you can get it back?"

"I hope so. I'm waiting to hear from them." And the wait was killing me.

"So, it was pure coincidence that you came into the station when I needed to see you?" He sounded skeptical.

"On this occasion, yes. No magic involved," I assured him. Reaching Bean Me Up, he held the door open for me and I stepped inside. It was quieter today, and we grabbed a table at the back.

"What are you having?" he asked. "It's on me."

"Thanks. I'll have a hot chocolate, please."

"Not a coffee drinker, then?"

"I am. I just really enjoyed the hot chocolate I had here yesterday." He was being super nice, and I wondered if he was buttering me up for something. Simon had deployed the same tactic, and to say I was a little gun-shy was an understatement.

He ordered our drinks, then sat opposite me, blowing out a breath. "Here's the thing," he said. "We know Whitney was poisoned. But the poison used is not in our database. Given your research capabilities, I was hoping you'd be able to help us try to identify it."

"Surely you need a chemist or scientist or something along those lines? Not a librarian."

"We've got a lab in East Dondure working on it, but I figured the more the merrier. Plus, you have an incentive to find the answer."

Crafty. Of course, I had incentive to find the answer if it would mean clearing my name.

"Is this ethical? I'm a suspect, after all."

"That's why I've got a lab in East Dondure working on it." His lips lifted in a grin and I was saved from answering by our drinks arriving. The waitress, a young, petite woman with golden blonde hair pulled into a ponytail, placed a hot chocolate in front of both of us and gave the detective a smile.

"Thanks, Lexi," he said, then waited until she'd left before picking up his cup and taking a cautious sip. "You're right," he said, "it's good. Well? What do you say?"

"How can I refuse?" I'd be a fool to say no, especially considering what he was asking was exactly what I wanted.

He paused with his mug halfway to his mouth, a flash of concern flickering across his face. "You have a choice," he pointed out. "I'm not forcing you. If you'd rather not..."

"No, no, I understand that," I blurted, realizing he'd misunderstood me. "It's just that after East Dondure, I was hoping for a fresh start. So far, it's not turning out so good."

"I understand." He nodded, but I seriously doubted that statement. Unless he'd been through something similar.

He chuckled. "Your face gives you away, Ms. Jones."

"Please call me Harper. The students called me Ms. Jones, and you're hardly a student."

"Harper, I know what it's like to feel you've lost it all. That your life is spinning out of control and that you've lost a grip on reality. It's terrifying. I get it."

"You do?"

"I do. I moved here for a fresh start, a do-over, just like you."

Some would consider it rude to ask. Not me. "What happened?"

He paused, then said, "I was shot in the line of duty." His words were devoid of emotion, but the pain and anguish in his eyes was impossible to miss. "My partner too. He died. I survived."

"Survivor's guilt?" I guessed, wanting to reach across the table and hold his hand. I held myself back. The last thing I needed was the detective to mistake my compassion for anything other than what it was.

"Pretty much. That whole '*if only we'd done this or taken that route*' or whatever. But we didn't. We spotted a stolen car, gave chase, and pulled it over. Cory reached the vehicle first, and the driver opened fire. Cory got hit in the chest, point blank, straight through his heart. He was dead before he hit the ground. I had enough time to duck for cover, although a bullet lodged in my hip."

"I'm so sorry," I whispered, my heart hurting for him. How awful.

He shook himself. "No, I'm sorry. I didn't mean to bring you down. I just wanted you to know you're not alone, that's all. This place, Whitefall Cove, it's kinda healing."

I nodded. "It is pretty special."

"So? You'll help?"

As if he had to ask. "Sure. I'll help." Rummaging in my purse, I pulled out a notebook and pen. "Tell me what you know about the poison."

"You always carry a notebook with you?" he asked, his surprise evident.

I looked down at the polka-dot-covered, dog-eared notebook that lived in my purse. "Doesn't everyone?" I grinned. "I'm a librarian. A lover of books." I shrugged. "I have notebooks everywhere."

He was right; they didn't have much to go on.

What was found in Whitney's stomach contents was an unknown substance that was toxic, yet they couldn't identify it. All they knew was that it had been ingested. And it was plant-based in origin.

"But you don't know how it killed her? How it worked?" I asked, tapping the end of my pen against my bottom lip.

He shook his head. "No. We won't know that until we identify what, exactly, it is. And that's where you come in."

"Remember, I'm a librarian, Detective Ward, not a scientist or biologist or an expert on anything, really." I felt it was only fair to warn him I might come up empty-handed, no matter how badly I wanted to find the answer.

"If I'm going to call you Harper, then you'd better call me Jackson."

"Why?" I blurted. "We're not friends. You don't have to be friendly toward me to ask for my help."

He leaned back in his chair and studied me before replying. "You're right. We're not friends. But that doesn't mean we can't be. And it's just a name. Call me whatever you want. I really don't care, but I figured you might have felt weird if I was using your first name and you were being formal, but if that's what you need to feel comfortable, whatever." He stood, dug into his pocket and laid a business card on the table. "Call me if you find out anything interesting."

He left me sitting at the table, feeling lousy and a tad defensive. Okay, so I was a little touchy, but I had reason to be. Simon had employed the same tactics to woo me—not that the detective was wooing me. He had a girlfriend; was dating his co-worker. He didn't have to employ any tactics whatsoever, and I was deflecting my experience with Simon onto him, which wasn't fair. I felt embarrassed that I'd reacted the way I had. He was being friendly. Full stop. Nothing more. It was me who was acting like a fool, and that rankled. I owed the detective an apology.

CHAPTER
FOUR

I ran to catch up with Detective Ward. Correction, Jackson.

"Wait!" I panted, sprinting to close the distance between us. He was almost at the corner, his long legs eating up the sidewalk faster than mine ever could. Hearing me yell, he glanced back over his shoulder, then stopped, waiting for me to catch up.

"First, I'm sorry if I sounded rude back there." I pressed a hand to my chest. Goodness, I was out of shape. I really needed to exercise more. A hundred-yard dash had my breath heaving in and out of my lungs and a sweat breaking out on my brow. "That's my bad and I apologize," I wheezed.

"No apology necessary," he said, waiting patiently while I caught my breath.

"Right. Because you weren't annoyed at all.

Anyway, whatever," I waved a hand in dismissal. "The second thing is, I need access to the books in my store. I know when I lived here before that Mr. Dudley had some remarkable old books. One of the first jobs on my list after purchasing The Dusty Attic was to do a stock take and see exactly what books are in stock and those that need to be ordered. But," I held up my hand when he opened his mouth to reply, "my whole rambling point is, I need access to the books for researching the poison that killed Whitney."

He grinned. "You should have led with that."

"Oh. So? You'll do it? I can finally have the keys to my store?"

"Shouldn't be a problem. Let me check whether forensics is done." He began walking again and pulled out his cell phone. I fell into step beside him. I had to go back to the police station anyway, since I'd left my car there.

"Liliana, hi." Oh, he was calling his girlfriend, the one who didn't like me. "Is forensics finished with The Dusty Attic? Swabs? Fingerprints? Photos?" There was a pause as he listened to her response, then in a super-calm tone, he replied, "Yes. I know you know how to do your job. I wasn't questioning it. I was asking if forensics was done." Silence again. I listened, unabashedly interested. Seemed Liliana was irritated at him for asking about the store. "I'm on my way back to the station now. Can you have the keys ready to sign out? And before you ask, yes, I am returning them to Harper Jones. She's helping me with something and needs access to the books." He winced and held the phone away from his ear, then glanced at me before cupping his hand over the phone and whispering, "She's on it."

Right. Whatever you say, champ. He hurried a few steps ahead and continued the conversation in a hushed whisper, and again I wondered what had Liliana so riled. I didn't know her; she didn't know me, yet by her reaction to my presence in the police station, she was not happy to see me *at all*. Of course, it probably didn't help that Jackson and I had just had hot chocolate together and now he was telling her to give me back my keys to the store—the one thing I'd gone in and asked for. Maybe she felt like he'd undermined her, and I could sympathize somewhat. It still didn't explain Liliana's hostility toward me.

When we returned, she was seething. Jackson left me at the counter, disappearing into his office and leaving us to it. I signed where she stabbed her finger on the clipboard she shoved across the counter. She slapped the keys down, then snatched the clipboard back without saying a word. Curling my fingers around the keys, I left with a muttered, "thanks."

It was a bittersweet moment. As I sat in my car, I opened my fist and looked at the keys nestled in my palm. My future. My very own bookstore. Butterflies swirled through my belly and a thrill of excitement shot through me. Today was the day the rest of my life started, and I couldn't wait. Despite what had happened with Whitney, I was still excited to find out where this new future would take me.

It took me twelve hours. Twelve short hours to identify what had killed Whitney. I seriously hadn't thought I'd find anything. After all, what did I have that a modern lab didn't? A hundred-year-old book on herbs, apparently.

I'd initially been disappointed when I scanned the shelves and discovered Mr. Dudley no longer stocked the old books I'd loved. That disappointment had turned to elation when I found them carefully packed away in a box in the storeroom, each book wrapped in special, moisture-resistant paper. I'd carried the box out to my car and taken it home. I'd much rather sift through the pages in front of a roaring fire on Gran's sofa than in the still-chilly bookstore.

"Got you!" I yelled, startling Gran, who was dozing in an armchair. A beam of magic shot out of her wand, bounced off the wall, and zapped me on the foot. I yelped.

"Oops," I said, clutching the herb book I'd discovered to my chest. "Sorry I woke you."

"Lord almighty, child!" Gran protested, stroking her wand as if to soothe it and placing it carefully on the side table next to her. "Serves me right for dozing off with that on my lap."

I rubbed at the top of my foot where my skin tingled from the shock. "You're okay," Gran assured me. "There was nothing but static electricity in the charge. Now tell me, what did you find?"

"Look, here." I opened the book and pointed. "Borrio bud. It looks like a hybrid between nightshade and hemlock. While nightshade contains atropine, which paralyzes muscles, hemlock contains conium, which paralyzes the respiratory system."

"So, what does borrio bud paralyze?" Gran asked.

"The heart. It specifically targets the heart. And while nightshade and hemlock will produce other symptoms such as nausea, and the onset is gradual, with borrio bud it looks like if you ingest it you won't know about it until your heart stops. About an hour later."

Gran leaned back in her chair. "Perfect if you want to kill someone, then. But if it's such a perfect poison, why have we never heard of it? Why aren't people using it all the time?"

"It only grows in the Amazon jungle."

"So how did someone in Whitefall Cove get their hands on a toxic plant that only grows in the Amazon jungle?"

"That's an excellent question. One that is going to take a lot more research." Closing the book, I yawned, glancing at my phone to check the time. "Gran! It's two in the morning! Why didn't you go to bed?"

"Because I dozed off in the chair," she replied, levering herself up with a creak of her bones. "But now that you've solved one part of the mystery, I'm going to bed. You should do the same."

Gran shuffled off, but I stayed slouched on the sofa, staring into the dying flames in the fireplace. Whoever wanted Whitney dead had knowledge about plants, specifically the borrio bud. What I needed was a list of suspects. Pulling out my notebook, I turned to a new page and started my list.

Who had I seen in the office the morning I met with Whitney? The receptionist, Christina. And Whitney's husband, Bruce, had dropped in to deliver her phone. Then there was her boss, Mike Palmer. I pondered the list before putting a number one next to Bruce's name. How many times had we seen it in the movies, in books, and even in real life—when a woman was murdered, it was almost always the husband? I needed to talk with him, and I had the perfect cover. He was Whitefall Cove's bank manager, and I needed to open a business account for The Dusty Attic. In the morning, I'd call and make an appointment, but for now, I needed sleep.

"Good to see you again, Harper." Bruce Sims shook my hand and ushered me into his office. He was a big man, older than Whitney, with laugh lines fanning out from his eyes. His skin was darker too, like he'd just returned from a Florida vacation.

"I wasn't sure you'd be at work." I took the seat he indicated and watched while he seated himself behind his enormous desk.

"I'd rather be busy than sitting at home twiddling my thumbs and driving myself crazy wondering who did this to her." His words were tinged with sadness, but something was missing, something I couldn't quite put my finger on.

"I guess," I nodded. "I'm sorry about Whitney. I mean, I know we weren't the best of friends but..." I trailed off with a shrug.

"Yeah, I understand. And thank you. The truth is, Whitney was mean to you because she was jealous." His revelation surprised me.

"What? Jealous? Of me? I cannot fathom why. My life is a wreck!"

"At school she wanted to be like you, smart, friendly, pretty. Slim. And the more she tried, the more it backfired, and she turned into the mean girl because it was easier to get what she wanted by bullying everyone else into giving it to her." He stood and looked out the window. "She mellowed somewhat over the years."

"Wow," I said quietly. "I never knew that. That's kinda..." I trailed off. The words *messed up* were on the tip of my tongue.

"Sad?" he supplied, his voice grim. "Isn't it though?" He sighed. "She was anxious about having you as a client. Even though she was delighted that your life in East Dondure imploded, she was nervous that you'd returned home. And then you bought The Dusty Attic."

"I don't get it," I admitted. "High school was a long time ago. Why would she be nervous that I'd moved back home? My being here in Whitefall Cove would have very little impact on her life."

He shrugged. "To Whitney, everything is a competition. *Everything*. You coming home, buying a bookstore, reminded her of her own failure."

"Failure?" I quizzed. From where I sat, Whitney had a pretty good life.

"To open her own realtor business. Mike was good enough to allow her to run it part time through his office while she worked there as his office manager, but it had been her dream to open her own place."

"Why didn't she?"

He shrugged. "I think she was so afraid of failing that she failed to launch. I'd done the numbers for her. There's demand. She could have made it a success. But in the end she was too scared to try, so she stayed in her comfortable rut as office manager for Palmer Construction."

We both lapsed into silence, pondering the enigma that was Whitney Sims. I had no idea she'd felt that way about me, and I would never have pegged her as a non-starter.

"She was happy, though, wasn't she?" I asked. "She had friends. And you. And hobbies? The two of you must have done stuff together, you know, like gardening?" I silently applauded myself on my segue into the *real* reason I was here.

"Gardening?" His brows shot up and he barked out a laugh. "Hardly. Whitney and I both have black thumbs and zero interest in gardening. We pay someone to mow our lawn."

I frowned. It was hardly likely that Bruce had been cultivating borrio bud. I got the sense that he genuinely missed his wife, but he wasn't as heartbroken as I'd expected. I recognized the signs. He was sad, for sure, but not brokenhearted. He was doing his best to play the grieving widower, but turning up to work the day after your wife is murdered was not what I'd consider normal behavior.

"So, what brings you in today?" Bruce broke the silence, leaning back in his chair and directing the conversation back to the business at hand. I explained I needed a business account for my bookstore. And an electronic banking system to accept payment from customers since I knew nothing about how they worked. I'd only ever been on the consumer side of the transaction and this "owning my own business" thing was a whole new world to me.

"How much working capital do you have?"

"Working capital?" I frowned, and he smiled indulgently. "How much cash do you have to get you started? That will determine if you need an overdraft account where you can dip into extra funds as and when you need, or a basic checking account if you don't require an overdraft facility."

For the next half hour, we talked business, and it was enlightening. Bruce Sims knew his stuff. He recommended a bookkeeper to me, a woman who kept the books for several of the bank's customers and wouldn't steer me wrong, he promised. I settled on an overdraft facility since I'd borrowed the money from Gran to purchase the store outright, but left myself with no working capital other than my personal savings and the ten thousand from selling my engagement ring. I'd wanted to put that toward the purchase of the store, but Gran had insisted she'd cover the cost and I could pay her back in installments when I could afford to.

I left the bank armed with all I needed to open my business, but none the wiser as to who killed Whitney.

CHAPTER
FIVE

"She said what?" Jenna, Monica and I had arranged to meet at The Dusty Attic and I was filling them in on what Officer Miles had said to me when I'd dropped into the police station to discuss my findings with Jackson.

"She said that suspects that insinuated themselves into an investigation are psychopaths," I repeated, nodding my head and agreeing with their outrage. It *was* outrageous. Clearly, Officer Miles disliked me. If only I knew why. Did she really think I was a murderer, responsible for Whitney Sims's death?

"Did you tell her Jackson asked for your help?" Monica said, snagging a straight-backed chair from the storeroom and straddling it, crossing her arms across the back. Jenna and I sat on the sofa in the reading corner of the store.

"We both did, and that seemed to make matters worse. What is it with the women in Whitefall Cove?"

"*I* know," Jenna said smugly, eyeballing me. "It's because a gorgeous, suddenly-single woman has moved back to town. They're jealous."

"Threatened, you mean," Monica added. "They're scared you're going to steal their men."

"What? No way! I'm done with men," I protested.

"I didn't say it was true. But it happens a lot. Women can be best friends one minute and then one of them suddenly becomes single and the other woman is threatened, thinks her friend is going to target her man. Makes up all sorts of ridiculous stories in her head." Monica sounded like she was speaking from experience.

I snorted, shaking my head in bafflement. "Well, they can't have very strong relationships then. I am not interested in any men in Whitefall Cove."

"Not even Detective Dreamy?" Monica teased.

I shook my head. "Not even. He's nice. I like him. But I'm not interested in him romantically. And he's not interested in me that way either," I pointed out. "You know," I pondered, tapping my chin, "Bruce said something similar. About Whitney."

"You've been talking with Bruce Sims?" Jenna asked.

Shrugging my shoulders to loosen the tightening of the gathering knots, I nodded. "I went in to arrange accounts for this place. I met with Bruce and he pointed me toward a bookkeeper who can help. And the right type of account I need. I don't mind admitting I'm in a little over my head with this."

"What did he say? About Whitney?" Monica asked.

"That she was jealous of me and that's why she was so mean when we were teenagers. And that she was nervous about having to deal with me when I came home."

"That's weird," Jenna said. "Like, why would she feel threatened by you? She and Bruce have been married for over ten years. Why would she think he would stray with you? No offense," she tacked on.

"None taken. And I've no idea why Whitney felt that way. Or if she really felt that way at all. I've only got what Bruce told me to go on. Which brings me back to why I called you here." Struggling up out of the old sofa, I crossed to the wall where a map of the world was suspended from a roller. With a tug, it rolled up, revealing a pin board hidden behind it.

"What's this?" Monica asked.

"A crime board." I smiled. "I'm going to get to the bottom of Whitney's murder, and you two are going to help me. You know how I told you Jackson asked for my help to identify the poison that killed her? Well, I found it. A rare plant that only grows in the Amazon. It's a combination of nightshade and hemlock called borrio bud and it specifically targets—and paralyzes—

the heart. And get this, it looks a hell of a lot like mistletoe."

"That is so cool," Monica said, and I smiled a little. She'd always been macabre, but I figured that came hand in hand with being a vampire.

"Not only in the Amazon," Jenna said, looking at the sticky note I'd pinned to the board with the words borrio bud written on it.

"Oh? You know about the borrio bud?" I wish I'd thought to ask Jenna, a Fae gardening genius and a journalist with a vast network of useful resources, instead of spending hours bent over an old book.

"I grow it. In my greenhouse," she said.

You could have knocked me over with a feather. "What?" I squeaked.

"Oh please, I don't grow it to poison people. I harvest the berries, crush them into a paste, and add soda and urine. I then use that as fertilizer on my lilies. Not only do they produce more flowers, but they also stay in bloom longer. The combination of carbonation, sugar, urea, uric acid and creatinine take out all traces of poison."

"Whose urine?" Monica asked, her gaze drilling into Jenna, who blushed. "Oh gross. It's yours, isn't it? You're peeing on your plants!"

"I am not peeing on my plants!" she objected, her cheeks red. "I pee in a pot and then store it in a jar in the fridge."

"Remind me not to eat or drink anything from your fridge ever again," Monica teased.

"Well, now I feel deflated," I said, perching on the arm of the sofa and looking at my forlorn crime board. My borrio bud discovery hadn't been the breakthrough I'd thought.

"Hey," Jenna protested, rubbing my back, "you did good. Few people know about the borrio bud, and for good reason. It *is* seriously toxic. And I'm not sure if anyone knows how to use it the way I do. I certainly haven't told anyone; this is my little secret. Well, to be honest, I learned it from my fellow Fae, but we certainly don't share the knowledge outside of the Fae community. It's a dangerous plant, after all."

"We should check your plant is all safe and sound and not missing any stems or leaves," Monica pointed out. "Because unless you're the murderer, I'd say someone used your plant to kill Whitney. I mean, what are the chances someone else in this town knows how to grow an exotic toxic plant?"

"Other members of the Fae community?" Jenna pointed out, but then frowned. "However, I'm pretty sure I'm the only one growing it. But I'll check with them."

"Before we do that, I want your help on something else," I told them. "I've made up a suspect list of who was in the Palmer Construction office the morning she died. Jenna, you can see their office from the *Tribune's* building. Did you see anyone else enter the day of the murder?"

"Who have you got?" she asked.

I pinned four names on the board, including my own.

"You, Christina Wallace, Bruce Sims and Mike Palmer. So, what are you wanting here? Opportunity? Alibi?"

"Anything really," I said. "I was standing next to Whitney when Christina came in with takeout coffees. She put them on the reception desk. Whitney didn't take hers, not when I was there. Mike took one and left. Bruce came in, gave Whitney her phone, and left immediately. I don't see how anyone could have poisoned her at that point."

"Borrio bud has to be ingested? Taken orally?" Monica asked Jenna.

She nodded. "Touching the plant with your bare hands, even having the leaves brush your skin, can lead to skin irritation, but it's the berries that are deadly."

She turned her attention to me. "Are you thinking the poison was in the coffee?"

I shrugged. "It could have been. Now that the police know what they're searching for, I'm hoping Jackson will keep me in the loop with whatever the lab finds."

Jenna played with a strand of hair. "Let me think. The takeout coffees came from Bean Me Up, correct?"

"Yes. I remember seeing the logo on the side of the cups."

"So we can't discount whoever made them—the barista—that's another suspect."

I scribbled the word barista on a sticky note and added it to the board. "Anything else?"

"I'm pretty sure I saw Wendy Haley outside the office that morning," Jenna said, "carrying a basket of baked goods—well, I assume they were baked goods. She does that a lot, whips up massive batches of muffins and what not and drops them off to Whitney or takes them to work with her."

"So, she and Whitney are still best friends, then? Where does she work?" I added her name to the board.

"She's a nurse. She arrived as Bruce was leaving. I saw them talking out front."

"I didn't see her at all, so she must have come in after Whitney and I went into her office." I tossed a marker at Monica. "Monica, can you start a timeline for me?"

"Sure. Got paper? Because I am not sticking a hundred Post-its together."

"I think I saw a roll of brown wrapping paper in the storeroom, left over from when Mr. Dudley used to hand wrap the books he'd sold."

Within seconds Monica was back with a long sheet of brown paper she taped to the wall below the pinup board.

"Start at me finding her dead and work backward," I instructed, watching as Monica drew a line along the paper and at the end wrote: Whitney dead ten a.m.

"Now what?" she asked.

"We add in the things we know. I met her at nine in her office. Put that in the middle. Christina came in with the coffees around the same time. And then Bruce dropped in and then Mike turned up. We need to find out her movements before she came to work and if she drank or ate anything, and what she was doing between nine and ten."

"And the other little mystery within the mystery," Monica muttered, diligently writing all the information on the timeline.

"Oh?"

"The keys to this place. She should have given them to you at your meeting at nine, but they were missing, which is why you arranged to meet her here later. Was that part of the plan? To make sure Whitney died away from the office and not at her desk?"

"Good point!" I scribbled the word keys on a sticky note and added it to the board.

"This is going to be fun!" Jenna examined the board, a smile on her face.

"Promise me you won't leak any of this? I know it's

an epic story, and God knows you're a brilliant journalist, but..." I trailed off. If the story broke, we'd tip the killer off.

Jenna signaled locking her lips and tossing away the key. "I promise I won't breathe a word. Providing, of course, I get to break the story when we catch the murderer."

"Well, duh, of course you will."

We were interrupted by a flash of light and a puff of smoke. An elf appeared, waving his arms to dispel the haze. "Fudgesickle. Magdalene said she'd fixed that," he grumbled, straightening his bow tie and smoothing his hair. "Harper Jones?" He peered at me and I glanced from him to Monica, then Jenna. *What was going on here?*

"Yes?" I eventually answered, since it was apparent he wasn't going to speak until I confirmed my identity. He handed me an envelope, bowed from the waist, then strode out of the store, muttering about how he was going to have it out with Magdalene and the teleport system that was *supposedly* fixed.

We all stared at his back and then down at the envelope. What the heck had I just been handed? And who the heck was Magdalene?

"What is it?" Monica peered at the envelope that had my name emblazoned on the front in a flowing gold font that glowed and sparkled on the paper. "And who was that?"

"I think he's from Drixworths," Jenna supplied. "And that," she nodded at the envelope, "is likely about your license."

"Oh." Monica leaned back as if it was toxic.

Turning the envelope over in my hands, I saw the green wax seal on the back with the Drixworths emblem stamped into it. "It is," I whispered, my heart thundering and anxiety sweeping through me. This was it. This was my further instruction. This would tell me if my magic license was gone forever.

My hands shook. "I can't look." Shoving the envelope

into my bag, I pulled the map down over the crime board to hide it before turning to Monica and Jenna, who were both staring at me with their mouths open.

"What?" I said defensively. "I'll look at it later, okay?"

"Harper," they said in unison.

Then Jenna added, "You should go home. Read it with your Gran. She'll know what to do."

"Yeah." Monica nodded. "We can go check on Jenna's plant and let you know what we find. You go home."

"But..." I tried to think up an excuse to put off the inevitable.

"Go!" Again, they spoke in unison and both of them pointed at the front door. Kicked out of my store, I sullenly trudged outside, waiting for them to join me.

"I've got work in an hour," Monica said once we were all outside. "We've gotta make this quick."

It was dark out and bitterly cold. I could feel the chill creeping up my legs, making me shiver.

"Plenty of time," Jenna replied, then wrapped me in her arms and squeezed me tight. Monica joined in the embrace, wrapping her arms around me from behind. "I hope it's good news," she whispered in my ear, then the two of them headed off, leaving me standing on the sidewalk feeling numb. I must have climbed into my car and driven home, for the next thing I knew I was standing in Gran's kitchen with no idea how I'd gotten there.

"It arrived then?" Gran bustled into the kitchen and I quickly covered my eyes with my hand.

"Gran!" I squeaked. "For heaven's sake, cover up, will you!"

"What?" she protested. "It's a negligee, Harper. Nothing wrong with that." I could feel her moving nearby, heard her fart and shook my head in resignation. Her negligee was red, lacy, and see-through. I'd seen more than my eyeballs could stand.

"You could have at least put panties on," I muttered, and she snorted.

"Why? I'll just be taking them off as soon as Derek arrives."

"Who the heck is Derek?" I dropped my hand from my eyes and stared at her, hard, keeping my gaze pinned on her face. "Your boyfriend?"

"One of them," she answered unapologetically, then seeing my face threw her hands up in the air. "Okay, fine." She waved her wand—I did not want to think where she'd been keeping it—and was soon wrapped head to toe in a fluffy purple dressing gown. "Geez, I don't remember you being this prudish," she grumbled.

"Who is Derek?" I repeated, not appeased in the slightest.

"Open the envelope," she demanded. We locked eyes, and I knew I was going to lose this battle.

"Fine!" I snapped, slapping the envelope on the kitchen table before taking a seat.

Gran didn't gloat, just sat in the chair opposite and waited. She looked from me to the envelope and back again. "Well? Get to it. I'm not getting any younger here."

Picking it up, I tore open the seal and unfolded the parchment inside. I quickly scanned the words, then looked up at Gran, a smile tugging at my lips.

"What's it say?"

"That I'm to undergo a refresher course at Drixworths and then they will reassess my license."

"Well, that's good news," Gran said, then stood, hustling out of the kitchen without another word. I conference-called Monica and Jenna with the news.

"That is fantastic." I could hear the joy in Jenna's voice, knew she was happy for me.

"It's a weight off my shoulders, that's for sure," I agreed. "Now tell me, how did it go on your end? Is your borrio bud plant intact?"

"It's not," Monica cut in. "Some low life has stolen the entire thing!"

"The whole plant is gone?" I gasped.

"Afraid so." Jenna sounded on the verge of tears. "I don't understand how the killer could have known about it. And to steal the whole plant? That could kill a lot of people."

"This is not your fault," I reassured her. "You weren't growing it for nefarious reasons. But someone found out about it, that's for sure."

"I've gotta get to work, babes," Monica said apologetically. "Let me know if there's anything I can do to help. In the meantime, I'll keep my ear out at Brewed Awakening, see if anyone lets anything slip."

After Monica disconnected, Jenna sniffed into the phone, "I swear I didn't tell anyone about the borrio bud, Harper."

"I know you didn't," I assured her. "You're far too careful for that. Does anyone have access to the greenhouse?"

"No. But it's not under lock and key or anything. It's just in my back garden, so anyone could have snuck in."

"You said only the Fae community knew about it? Was there anyone specifically who knew, for sure? Maybe they let it slip unintentionally?"

"No one springs to mind," Jenna replied. She'd gone from sounding distraught to determined. "I'm going to get to the bottom of this, mark my words. I refuse to break this story from a jail cell." She paused for a second. "Although that could catapult me to the front page."

I chuckled. "I don't think that's the front-page coverage you want, hon."

"You know what they say. Any publicity is good publicity."

After finishing the call with Jenna, I headed to bed, wanting to be well rested for my first class at Drixworths. I was extremely grateful for the soundproof spell Gran placed on her room, keeping any of the noise she got up to with her current beau, Derek, to herself. A girl did not need to know her eighty-year-old grandmother was getting more action than her.

Despite that, I tossed and turned all night. Part nerves about Drixworths, and part distraction because of Jenna's missing plant. Jenna swore she'd told no one, so how had the killer found out about it? A question I was still pondering at breakfast.

Sipping my coffee, I called Jackson, wanting to bring him up to speed and plead with him, if necessary, not to arrest Jenna. There was no way she was the killer. I refused to even entertain the possibility. The only feasible answer was that the killer stole the plant. Which really didn't get me any further ahead. I still had no idea who that was.

When Jackson didn't answer, I left him a voice mail, then got ready for my first class at Drixworths.

Parking in the lot outside the Academy, I studied the towering mansion. This was not Hogwarts, that's for sure, but having said that, this wasn't Drixworths Academy of Witchcraft and Wizardry's head office. That was in East Dondure and I was kicking myself that I'd never visited, not once, during my time in the city. The building before me now was merely Whitefall Cove's branch of Drixworths. Even so, it was epically spectacular.

Walking up the front path, I could feel the magic swirling around me and getting stronger with each step toward the massive front doors. I thought I was alone, my feet the only footsteps crunching on the gravel path until suddenly there was a hoard of witches practically stampeding toward the door, looming up behind me and jostling as they pushed past, excited and eager to get inside. I followed more sedately, acknowledging to myself that it was slightly humiliating to be attending class at my age, but if this was what it took to get my license back, I'd suck it up and do it.

"Ms. Jones." I was greeted at the door by the same elf who'd appeared in my bookstore last night. "The headmistress would like to see you before class. This way, please."

I followed him. He was all of three feet tall and wobbled from side to side as he walked. He vetoed the massive staircase dominating the entrance for a hallway running parallel to it. We passed dozens of closed doors before coming to one at the rear of the building. Etched on the frosted glass pane was the name Esmerelda Higginbottom, Headmistress. With a light knock, he swung the door open and ushered me inside.

"Harper." Esmeralda Higginbottom did not live up to her name. I'd expected a grizzled old witch with gray hair and a wart on her nose. In front of me stood a svelte redhead, with flawless skin, and the shine on her hair had me green with envy.

Remembering my manners, I stepped forward with my hand outstretched. "Harper Jones, pleased to meet you, Ms. Higginbottom."

The gentle tinkling sound of her laugh was as divine as her beauty. "Please, call me Izzy. My parents lumbered me with a mouthful of a name. Izzy is easier for everyone." She shook my hand and then indicated the chair in front of her desk. "I won't keep you long. Please, have a seat." She waited until I was seated before she resumed her own, lowering herself so gracefully onto her chair it was as if she were liquid.

She smiled. "I'm delighted the head office has agreed to give you a second chance," she began, tilting her head as she talked. "I've reviewed your case myself and I don't believe your actions were intentionally malicious. Purely an unguided, unintended reaction to the circumstances in which you found yourself."

My lips thinned at the reminder, but she wasn't wrong.

"That being said, you need to keep control at all times. Your magic will be made available to you temporarily while on the Drixworths premises, but once you set foot outside, you will lose it again. Also, you have been assigned a familiar. This is non-negotiable and permanent. Your familiar will help control your magic and should you lose control of your powers, he can intercept for you."

Having a familiar meant having a creature tied to me for the rest of my life and, while I had nothing against it *per se*, it wasn't something I'd ever considered in the past. Then again, if that was what Drixworths wanted, then I'd happily accept a familiar.

"Meet Archie." A striped ginger cat jumped down from the windowsill with a meow and padded across the floor toward me, his big round eyes golden.

"Archie, huh?" I reached down my hand to the feline who sniffed my feet and rubbed himself around my ankles with a purr. "Aren't you the handsome one?"

He jumped onto my lap with a meow, turned in a circle, then settled in for a nap. I smiled, already finding his presence comforting. I stroked his fur as Izzy continued talking.

"I'll keep a close eye on your progress and when I think you're ready, you'll sit an exam. Pass it and your witch's license will be returned. Fail, and," she paused, leveling a stern look my way. "Let's just say we will have to reassess at that point." There was a thread of steel in her voice, a hidden warning behind her words. I got the sense if I failed that exam, she would take it personally and would not be pleased.

"Bring Archie with you to every class," she instructed. "It is important he knows your strengths and limitations with magic."

"I will. Thank you."

"You can go." She dismissed me with a wave of her hand and turned her attention to a pile of papers stacked on her desk. With a click of her fingers, her pen began signing them.

Scooping Archie into my arms, I cuddled him to my chest. "Come on, Archie, let's go."

The elf was waiting for me outside and guided me back along the hallway, up the grand staircase to a classroom on the left.

"Nice of you to finally join us, Ms. Jones." Another stunningly beautiful witch stood at the head of the class, her supermodel good looks hard to tear my eyes from. I felt positively frumpy in comparison and wondered if the witches at Drixworths were spelled to appear more attractive than they were.

"A fine observation," the witch said, pointing to a table at the front of the class where she could keep an eye on me like a naughty child. *Great. A mind reader teacher. Just what every student wants.* I heard sniggers from my classmates as I made my way down the center aisle and slid into the seat indicated. Archie curled himself back onto my lap and promptly returned to his slumber.

"Let me recap for the tardy Ms. Jones," the witch said, and I wanted to argue that it was hardly my fault I was late—I was in a meeting with the headmistress —but bit my lip and stayed silent. These people were assessing me, deciding if I was worthy of my witch's license. It would not bode well for me if I was argumentative on day one, but who knew what tomorrow would bring?

"My name is Phyllis. I'll be teaching you basic spell casting and harnessing the magic of your wand. Since the rest of the class has already introduced themselves, I'll save them the bother from having to do it again. Everyone, this is Harper Jones. Let her be an example of what not to do. She's here because she had her witch's license suspended."

I glared at Phyllis, anger making my cheeks flush, but I kept silent even as sniggers and whispers filled my ears. She'd done it on purpose, and I was determined not to rise to the bait. The whole town of Whitefall Cove knew what had happened. It wasn't a surprise to anyone in this room, so I saw no reason why Phyllis was rubbing it in, other than to get me to snap. I was determined not to.

"And as Harper observed upon entering this room, my appearance is very much affected by magic." With a wave of her wand, she changed before our eyes from a stunning supermodel to a rather ordinary woman, a little plumpish, with mousy brown hair. "I was using an enhancement spell."

Hands shot up around the room and I could predict what the questions would be. They all wanted to learn the spell so they could get around looking like supermodels. What they didn't realize was that such a spell drained your magic. You couldn't maintain it for long periods of time, and as a witch new to your powers, you could probably hold it for a minute or two, tops.

"Correct again, Harper." Phyllis nodded at me in approval.

"You're a mind reader," I said. So, she'd have heard my internal monologue on keeping my temper, not letting her rile me.

"Correct on both counts. And before you ask—no, this is not what it's going to be like the entire time you're here." Addressing the rest of the class, she instructed, "Turn to chapter one of your spell books."

There was no spell book on my desk. I glanced around. Everyone else flipped to the relevant page. "Here." The girl at the desk next to me handed me a spell book. "Some others thought it would be funny to hide yours. I took it for safekeeping. I figure this is hard enough for you without them playing tricks."

I accepted the book and smiled. "Thanks, I appreciate it."

"I'm Alayna Temple." She reached out her hand and I shook it.

"Hi, Alayna. I'm Harper. This is Archie." I indicated the orange fur ball asleep on my lap.

"Cool, you have a familiar?" She leaned over and scratched the top of Archie's head. He cracked open one eye, looked at Alayna, purred, and closed his eye again.

"A necessity, it seems." I shrugged. "I take it you're a first year?"

"I am." She nodded enthusiastically, and I knew that Alayna Temple was not only a good person, but she was going to make an awesome witch.

"You have a raw talent." Phyllis, our instructor, appeared at my shoulder.

"Oh?"

"You can read people and situations."

"Yeah well, I didn't read a certain person in East Dondure very well," I muttered. Simon's betrayal had come as a complete surprise to me.

"Oh, I think you knew. You just didn't want to know. So, you ignored what was in front of you until it became impossible to ignore. It's my job to train you to trust your instincts. You have good, powerful magic, Harper. You've got to put your faith in it, believe in it, and it won't steer you wrong."

Phyllis moved to the front of the class again and clapped her hands. An apple appeared on each of our desks. "Right, witches and wizards," Phyllis said, smiling, "today we are going to make this apple look like a banana. We will not change it into a banana. We are going to glamor it, so it simply looks like one. Wands ready? And begin!"

It was good to feel the magic in my wand again, feel the power tingle where my fingers wrapped around it. With a tap of my wand on the apple, it immediately took on the appearance of a banana as requested. Of course, it was easy for me. I'd done all of this before, and I questioned whether putting me in a beginner class was of much benefit.

Phyllis must have read my mind again, because she leaned down and said into my ear, "It's for their benefit, not yours. Today you are to be paraded as an example of what not to do. I'm sorry, I know that feels rough. But after this class, you'll be in an advanced group or one-on-one tuition."

As the class went through the basics, I thought about what Phyllis had told me, that I had talents in reading people. It wasn't a skill I'd ever considered having before, but now I couldn't help but think how handy it would be to catch a murderer. I didn't miss the sly grin Phyllis threw my way as she helped a student who had smashed her apple into a messy pulp on her desk. This could be very helpful indeed.

CHAPTER
SEVEN

Jackson was waiting out front of Drixworths when classes dismissed at lunchtime. Cradling Archie to my chest, I ambled down the gravel path to where he was leaning against his car, feet crossed at the ankles, arms crossed over his chest. Seeing me, he pushed into an upright position and waited.

"I've been calling you," he said by way of a greeting, and my eyes widened.

"You have? My phone didn't ring." I tried to hold Archie with one hand and dig around in my purse for my phone with the other, but it was useless.

Seeing my struggle, Jackson reached across and plucked Archie from my arms. "Here. I'll take the cat."

"His name is Archie," I told him, retrieving my phone. Sure enough, three missed calls from Jackson.

"That's odd. I'm sorry, I wasn't ignoring you. It didn't ring, I swear."

He shrugged. "Doesn't matter. So you said you had news? Big news?"

"Yes!" I took Archie back and told him about the borrio bud plant Jenna had been cultivating in her greenhouse and how it was now missing.

"So we might have the murder weapon," he mused, running his hand around the back of his neck as he pondered what I told him. "Where did Jenna get the plant from? Did she purchase it? Buy seeds?"

"I'm afraid you'll have to ask her all of that. I've no idea." I narrowed my eyes at him. "But she's innocent in all of this."

"That may well be, but she was growing a highly poisonous plant that someone has now stolen. She's involved, like it or not."

"It's not illegal to grow borrio bud. Is it?" I really hoped I hadn't just gotten Jenna into a whole heap of trouble.

He shrugged. "I don't know. I'll have to check into it."

Holy guacamole, this was all my fault. I'd dragged Jenna into this and now she might potentially face charges—that's if it turned out to be illegal to be growing a certain plant. My face must have reflected my thoughts because Jackson laid a hand on my shoulder in a comforting gesture and said, "She's not in trouble with the Whitefall Cove Police, if that's what has your face all scrunched up."

"Harper!" I was saved from answering by Gran, heading toward us in a skin-tight purple cat suit, leopard print scarf, an umbrella with yellow ducks held above her head despite the fact that it wasn't raining, and on her feet, the beloved Ugg boots, although this pair had been bedazzled to within an inch of their lives.

"I'll talk to you later." Jackson nodded at me, smiled a greeting at Gran, and climbed into his car. I watched as he drove away, then turned my attention to Gran, keeping my eyes glued to her face, for the purple fabric of her cat suit left little to the imagination and while I admired Gran's appreciation of her body, I didn't need to see quite so much of it.

"Hi, Gran, what brings you to Drixworths today?"

"Heard you had a familiar," she puffed, trudging up to us. Archie looked at her with wide orange eyes and when she stroked his head, he purred.

"This is Archie." I didn't resist when Gran took him from me and cuddled him to her chest, burying her face in his fur and whispering, "Who's a gorgeous boy, then?"

"And how did you hear that? I only got him a couple of hours ago."

"Witches' grapevine." She winked. "What are your plans for the rest of the day?"

"I'm going to The Dusty Attic. I need to get it ready to open. It's five days until Christmas and I'm hemorrhaging sales by keeping it closed." Not to mention, I wanted to spend some time pondering the latest developments regarding Whitney's murder.

"I'll help," she offered, and I looked at her in surprise.

"You don't have anything else on? Because you seem awfully dressed up for working in a bookstore."

"Oh, this old thing? I had yoga this morning."

I snort-laughed. "You did yoga in that? How? No! On second thought, don't tell me. I don't want to know. Come on then, I'll give you a ride."

The Dusty Attic was exactly that—dusty. Everything was covered in a fine layer of dust and cobwebs and I knew I had hours of cleaning ahead of me, let alone taking stock of what books were on hand. I'd need to get my hands on some newer titles if I was going to draw in the Christmas crowd. Gran set Archie on the floor and he immediately began exploring. I needed to buy pet supplies for my new familiar and get extra to bring in to the store since I imagined he'd be spending a lot of time here with me.

"Your thermostat is dodgy." Gran huffed, rubbing her hands up and down her arms.

"You're hardly dressed for the weather," I pointed out. But she was right—it was cold in the store, despite Jenna and I turning on the heating. "Let me go check. In the meantime, why don't you conjure up a coat?" I told her.

I opened the storeroom door and stepped inside, my breath appearing in a white cloud in front of my face. Gadzooks, it was freezing in here. Crossing to the thermostat, I frowned. It was off. Who had turned my heat off? As far as I knew, no one else had a key, and even if they did, why would they come in and turn off the heat? It made no sense. Turning the dial back on, and cranking the temperature up to high, I returned to Gran, who was now wrapped in a fur coat; her wrinkled face was the only part of her visible.

"Relax, it's not real fur," she chided.

"I didn't say anything," I protested.

"Oh please, you don't have to. Everything you think is written all over your face." She cocked her head, listening to the ailing heating system get to work. "You're going to want to get that looked at."

"I know," I sighed, digging around in my purse and pulling out my notebook. "I'm making a list. There's so much to be done. I'm worried I won't be able to open until *next* Christmas."

"Nonsense." She rubbed her hands together. "You may be hamstrung with no magic at the moment, but I'm here, fully loaded. Point me at what needs doing and I'll get it sorted for you, honey."

"Oh, Gran, thank you!" I beamed. "That's brilliant! I have a vision." Leaning my elbows on the counter, I told Gran how I pictured the store to be. A fantasy fairytale corner for children's books, with a place for story time. Magical bookcases that would know the perfect books for my customers and fill the shelves with them. Lots of comfy old chairs and sofas for reading. The ceiling—oh, the ceiling!—would be magnificent, changing upon the weather: glorious blue skies with puffy white clouds, sparkling stars in the night sky, spooky, heavy thunderclouds rolling across. And the interior of my bookstore would be like a cozy country cottage, depicting an attic filled with treasures.

"I can do all of that for you, child." She grinned, then held up a hand. "Except for the thermostat. You're on your own with that."

"That's fine, Gran. I'll make some calls and get someone in to check it."

"Tell you what, pop across the road and get me a double shot macadamia-almond milk latte, and by the time you get back, this place will be tickety-boo."

Snatching up my purse, I did as instructed. It was the least I could do. After all, Gran was saving me hours of backbreaking labor, and if she could recreate my vision for the store? It would be epic, for that plan had been put on hold thanks to my lack of magic. I'd been intending to give the store a thorough scrub, and that was pretty much it. Any renovations had been placed on the back burner until my witch's license was restored.

Standing in line at Bean Me Up, I watched out the window as a circle of magical stardust swirled over the roof of the Dusty Attic—the process was quite amazing.

"Good afternoon. What can I get you today?"

"Oh, sorry!" I'd been so entranced by what was happening across the street I hadn't noticed it was my turn to order. I smiled at the barista, the same young woman who'd served Jackson and me the other day. Her name badge said, Lexi.

She smiled warmly. "Not a problem. You're the new owner of The Dusty Attic?" She nodded her head toward the window.

"Yes. Harper Jones." I stuck out my hand, and she shook it, her grip firm. A little too firm. I winced, giving my hand a discreet shake once she released it.

"Lexi Sawyer," she replied. "I've seen you in here a few times now."

"Yes, well, my friend introduced me to your hot chocolates and I have to say, they are slightly addictive." I grinned.

"So, one hot chocolate?" she asked, grabbing a takeout cup and writing my name on it.

"And one double shot macadamia-almond milk latte, and one cup of warm milk, no froth, no additives." When she raised an eyebrow, I explained, "It's for my cat."

"Gotcha." She nodded, lining up the three cups, ringing up my order, then swiping my card. "Won't be long."

She got busy with the coffee machine and, true to her word, mere minutes later, she slid a cardboard tray toward me with three cups wedged in the allotted spaces.

"I'm guessing the macadamia-almond milk latte is for your Gran," she said conversationally. "She's the only one who orders it. Well, the only one who double-shots it."

"Yeah, Gran has eccentric tastes," I replied, not paying a lot of attention. I was keen to get back to my store and see what Gran had created for me. "So, you sell a lot of them then? Non-double-shot ones, that is?"

"Oh no. Only one other customer used to order it. She died," she added, wiping down the counter.

I narrowed my eyes, then glanced over my shoulder to make sure I wasn't holding up the line. I wasn't; I was the only one at the counter. "She died?"

"Yeah, Whitney Sims. It was her drink of choice. Not that she came in often, it was usually her assistant, Christina."

"And you're the one who usually made her order?"

Lexi shrugged. "Most days. Christina usually came

in sometime between eight thirty and nine. My shift starts at eight, so yeah, unless I'm on a day off, I tend to get the Palmer Construction orders. And I only remember it because of Whitney's order. So pretentious." Then she slapped a hand over her mouth. "I'm sorry—I don't mean to imply that your Gran is pretentious."

I chuckled. "She isn't. That's why hers is a double shot."

Lexi's lips curled into a smirk and she tucked a strand of her shoulder-length golden blonde hair behind one ear and leaned forward. "The gossip is, Whitney was murdered—well, I guess you know all about that since she was found in your bookstore and all." She rested her elbows on the counter and dropped her voice. "But I'm not surprised someone knocked her off. It was bound to happen, eventually."

"Oh?" Up close, Lexi's eyes were a mesmerizing shade of green, flecked with gold, and slanted slightly at the corners.

"She was rude to pretty much everyone in town. And when she bragged that she'd gotten a Christmas bonus and her assistant Christina—who, let's face it, probably did most of the work anyway—didn't, well, the yelling match between Christina and their boss could be heard all across town."

I leaned in, our heads almost touching, eager to hear more.

Lexi obliged. "I also heard that Whitney had something on her boss. Maybe she was sleeping with him or something, I don't know, but there was something other than an employer-employee relationship."

"You think Whitney was having an affair with Mike Palmer?" I tried, and failed, to keep the excitement out of my voice.

Lexi shrugged. "Can't say for sure. Just stuff I overheard here and there."

The bell above the door rang and a young man ambled up to the counter, standing in line behind me. I straightened and picked up my order. "Thanks for the chat, Lexi. It's been enlightening."

"Anytime, Harper." She smiled, then turned her attention to her next customer.

Hurrying out of the shop, I returned to The Dusty Attic, my mind a whirl. What if Whitney was having an affair with her boss, and her husband found out? That gave him a motive. It also gave her boss, Mike Palmer, a motive—what if things had turned sour? Or what if Whitney had promised to leave her husband and then reneged?

Opening the door to The Dusty Attic, I stopped on the threshold, my mouth dropping open. It was *amazing*.

"I tweaked your vision a little," Gran said, standing in the middle of the store with her hands on her hips and a smug look on her face. "You like it?"

"I love it!" I beamed. It was better than my vision. She'd created a mezzanine level with gilded railings and towering bookcases, complete with a ladder on a rail to reach the higher shelves. The walls were red brick with a dark mahogany bottom panel. My counter was now a vintage desk with a green banker's lamp and ornate till, a red upholstered chair behind it. Wall sconces matched the massive chandelier hanging from the ceiling, the candlelight flickering from it amazingly real. The once-tiled floors were now a dark hardwood, with a round rug in front of my desk. In the middle of the store, an old dresser with a coffee pot, a mug with pens stacked inside, and at the back, two elegant wing-back armchairs and a Chesterfield sofa faced an open fireplace where a fire crackled. The door to the storeroom had been hidden by a red velvet curtain. Antique stained-glass windows dominated the storefront, and books with wings were suspended from the rafters.

"Gran, this is amazing!" In a daze, I stepped forward and placed the cardboard takeout tray on the dresser, looking around, trying to take it all in.

Gran slung her arm around my shoulders. "I'm pretty pleased with it myself." Grabbing her drink, she took a mouthful and sighed. "Lexi made this, huh? Only she can make it this good."

"Yeah." I was distracted by my store, overwhelmed with how wonderful it looked. Then I spotted Archie, sitting on a rug in front of the fireplace. "Gran. What is he wearing?"

"Hmmm?" She glanced at Archie, who sat dressed in what looked like a Sherlock Holmes outfit, his tail flicking in what could only be annoyance. "Oh that. Cute, isn't he?"

"No, no costumes for my cat," I said, taking Archie's cup of warm milk and kneeling by his side. "Sorry, boy." I quickly removed his outfit, and he head-bumped me. I liked to think it was in thanks. "Here you go, Archie. I got you some milk." I flipped the plastic lid from the cup and set it on the floor before returning to Gran's side.

"Gran, I had a world map on the wall over there." I pointed to a wall that now sported heavy wooden bookshelves. "Any chance of getting it back?"

"Oh, you don't want that old map." She waved her hand in dismissal.

"I want what was behind it," I muttered, thinking of my crime board with the timeline and suspects for Whitney's murder.

"Oh, your murder board? I kept that. Here." With a snap of her fingers, the big heavy bookcase glided effortlessly to the side, revealing the crime board behind it.

"Thank you," I said, "but, Gran? I don't have

magic. I can't move the bookcase on my own. And I'm not calling you each time I want to move it."

"Relax, sugar plum, I thought of that. I spelled it. All you have to do is say *reveal* and it will move. When you're done, say *hide*, and it will move back. It'll only respond to your voice."

"Hide," I said, and sure enough, the bookcase slid effortlessly back into place, the crime board once more hidden from view. "And it's not a murder board," I muttered. "It's a crime board."

"Tomato potato," Gran replied. "Now tell me, what's got you all riled up? You came back from Bean Me Up vibrating with energy. And you want your crime board." She over-exaggerated the word, letting me know she thought the distinction between crime board and murder board was negligible. "You've got a lead, haven't you?"

CHAPTER
EIGHT

"I now call the Whitefall Cove book club to order." Gran conjured a gavel and banged it on the coffee table, making us all jump.

"Gran," I protested, "this isn't a book club."

"It isn't a bad idea though," Monica said. "I'd join. What books shall we read, Mrs. B?"

"Fifty Shades of Eat, Pray, Love," Gran replied, "and then Alice and Elvis's Adventures in Wonderland."

We laughed so hard it brought tears to my eyes. Trust Gran to mix and match book titles, much like she mixed and matched everything in life.

"Okay, fine," she huffed. "The Whitefall Cove murder club, then."

Monica screeched with laughter, holding her sides and rocking back and forth. The sound startled Archie, who'd been dozing in front of the fireplace but was now wide awake, his hackles raised.

"Gran." I shook my head at her and she shot me a cheeky grin. "Okay, okay, it's not such a bad idea," I relented. "A book club, that is. But, Gran, I am not reading *Fifty Shades of Grey* with you."

"Why on earth not?"

Jenna cleared her throat. "So, um, getting back to our discoveries?"

"Yes, you're right. Let's focus. *Reveal*," I commanded, and the bookcase moved as instructed. I'd already added the clues I'd discovered today, along with the note about Jenna's missing borrio bud plant.

"Lexi is the barista who made the coffees?" Jenna squinted at the board.

"Yes, she told me herself that she makes the usual takeout order for Palmer Construction. That Christina comes in every morning to collect it."

"That would mean anyone could watch the place for a while and pick up the routine," Monica said. "Intercept the coffee before it reached its destination."

"But how would you intercept—and add the poison—without being noticed?" I wondered.

"Wouldn't be easy," Jenna agreed.

We went through the rest of the clues I'd gathered. "Lexi insinuated something was going on between Whitney and Mike," I said.

"An affair?" Gran rubbed her hands together. "Now we're getting somewhere."

"Not necessarily," I cautioned. "She didn't say an affair, just that something was going on. Maybe it wasn't romantic?"

"A love triangle," Monica drawled, crossing a long leg over her knee. "How delightful."

"We need to find out for sure." Tapping my lip with my finger, I frowned at the board. I could ask Mike outright, but would I get the truth?

"The Whitefall Cove Christmas Party is tomorrow night," Jenna said. "What if we got each of them alone, did some digging? You've got a sticky note up there about Whitney's Christmas bonus, and what Lexi told you is true. I remember Christina and Mike having an awful row last week, right out in front of the office. I couldn't hear what they were saying, but there was a lot of arm action and they looked like they were shouting. Well, Christina did. Mike was shaking his head and rubbing his face like he was fed up with the whole thing."

"Interesting. Yes, all right. Jenna, you see if you can get Christina to open up about what the fight was about. I'll talk to Mike. See if I can get a sense if he had romantic feelings toward Whitney," I said.

"I'll talk to Bruce," Monica volunteered. "Maybe he knew his wife was having an affair. Or at least suspected."

"What about me?" Gran asked, sitting on the edge of her seat in anticipation. "Who shall I talk to?"

I thought hard for a minute. "How about Wendy, Whitney's best friend?" I suggested. "But remember, do not breathe a word of what we're doing here, okay? It's a secret."

"Pfft, what do you take me for?" Gran grumbled. "I'm not an idiot." There was silence for a moment, then she piped up with, "Why don't we want them to know?"

I shook my head. "Because we don't want to tip the murderer off that we're on to them."

Monica sniggered. "That's because we're not. We're throwing darts at a map."

"What map?" Gran looked around, confused.

"It's just a saying, Gran," I explained, "like throwing spaghetti at the wall, seeing what sticks."

"Oh, like how long is a piece of cake?"

I bit back a laugh. "Yes, exactly. So, remember, the book club is a secret."

"Gotcha." She winked.

"Harper, I'd like to join your book club, if that's okay?"

I did my utmost not to roll my eyes. Gran was telling everyone that I'd started a book club, forgetting entirely that the book club was a cover for our investigation into Whitney's murder. I'd had ten people in the last hour approach me, wanting to join. Plastering a smile on my face, I turned to Gloria Wheatley. "That's fantastic, Gloria. I'll add you to the list. I hope Gran told you I'm still in the planning stages? I want to get The Dusty Attic open first and then we'll look at scheduling our first meeting."

"Of course, no rush, but I wanted to say what a wonderful idea."

"Thank you. If you'll excuse me? I need to refresh my drink." I waved my empty glass and slipped away. The Whitefall Cove Christmas party was in full swing, the town hall packed. On the stage at one end of the enormous hall stood a massive Christmas tree, and the hall was decorated with boughs of holly and rather too much mistletoe for my liking. I suspected Gran had a hand in the decorations. She was a sucker for a stolen kiss beneath the mistletoe. Christmas carols pumped through the speakers and the atmosphere was festive.

"You look lovely this evening," Jackson said, appearing by my side. "Another?" He indicated my empty glass and when I nodded, he took it from me, scooping eggnog into it from the punch bowl on the trestle table laden with food.

"Thank you." Smiling, I accepted the glass. I'd worn a red lace dress that molded my upper body and flared out into a full skirt at the waist. I felt pretty and feminine in it and I was pleased with his compliment. "You don't look so bad yourself."

He laughed. "I look the same as always. I came straight from work."

"Oh? Got a break on the case?" I asked, taking a sip of the eggnog and coughing. Someone had added something extra since my last glass, and I had a sneaking suspicion I knew who the culprit was. I'd seen Gran hovering nearby only ten minutes ago and had thought she looked shifty. I bet she'd spiked it. With a mental eye roll, I tuned back into what Jackson was saying.

"I wish. Just busy this time of year." Someone jostled me from behind and he took my elbow to guide me off to one side. "I hear you're starting a book club?"

"Oh my God, I can't believe she's telling everyone!"

"Does that mean you aren't?"

"I wasn't, no. But Gran has gone and told everyone that I am, and people have been asking to join, which means now I have to start one."

"Well, you don't have to," he pointed out.

"How can I not?" I protested. "Seems this town is crying out for one. I had no idea, but maybe it'll help to get customers into The Dusty Attic if a book club goes along with it."

"Don't fret, you'll have a bunch of people sign up. About half of those will actually turn up and then, as time goes on, half of them will drop out," he predicted.

"Leaving me with a nice, manageable book club." I nodded, liking his logic.

"Exactly." He grinned.

"There you are!" We were interrupted by Officer Miles. I nearly didn't recognize her. Her hair, usually pulled back in a tight, unforgiving bun, now flowed in silken waves down past her shoulders. Her eyes were adorned with winged eyeliner, her lips a ruby red, and her dress? It was stunning. A figure-hugging silver sheath that clung to her curves all the way to her ankles, with a thigh-high split revealing just enough toned leg.

"Wow!" Jackson exclaimed, leaning in to kiss her cheek. She slid her hand around his arm, her smile content. "You look amazing." His words were for her alone, but I couldn't help but overhear them given I was standing right next to them.

"Thank you, babe," she breathed, fluttering her eyelashes. Then her gaze slid to me and a shutter came down over her features.

"Harper. That's a pretty dress," she said.

"Not as stunning as yours," I replied, giving her a warm smile. "You look absolutely beautiful."

She looked taken aback, so I raised my glass, said, "Merry Christmas," and hurried away, leaving them alone. I spied Jenna, who was jerking her head sideways and giving me frantic eye signals. I met her outside the ladies' bathroom.

"You'll never believe it," she whispered, clutching my arm and glancing furtively around to make sure we weren't overheard.

"What is it?" I whispered back.

"I got talking with Christina, and once I got a couple of eggnogs into her, well, let's just say her tongue was sufficiently loosened."

I cocked my head and looked at her suspiciously. "Did you tell Gran to spike the eggnog?"

She looked as guilty as sin but denied it, anyway. "I did not. But I saw her do it, so I used it to my advantage. Just be mindful that your Gran appears to be continually spiking the eggnog and I fear it will end up tasting like moonshine and strip the enamel from everyone's teeth by the end of the night."

"She's done this before." Blowing out a breath, I pinned Gran with a look across the room. Oh, she knew all right, giving me a cheeky grin and a shrug and then taking a hefty gulp of her eggnog, smacking her lips in appreciation. "What am I going to do with her?" I wondered out loud.

"She's certainly entertaining," Jenna said. "Anyway, back to Christina. She was more than happy to spill the beans on her fight with Mike—she's still furious with him about it."

"Why? What happened?"

"Apparently, he gave Whitney a ten thousand-dollar Christmas bonus!"

"What?" My head jerked back. That was a lot of money. A serious amount of money. No wonder Christina was mad.

"How much did he give Christina?" I asked.

"That's just it. *Nothing*. He doesn't give out Christmas bonuses. It's never been a thing with Palmer Construction. He gives every employee a one-hundred-dollar gift card every year at the holidays, but never a bonus, and never such an astronomical amount."

"I'd imagine Mike didn't want the others to know, so how did Christina find out?"

"Whitney told her. Bragged about it and rubbed her nose in it, apparently." Jenna mimed Whitney doing exactly that and I couldn't contain the laugh. She was alarmingly accurate at impersonating the realtor.

"So, another motive then." My suspect list wasn't getting any smaller. Money was a big motivator and Whitney could have pushed Christina too far with her bragging and showing off so much that Christina snapped and killed her. She had access to the coffees, had purchased them from Bean Me Up. Motive *and* opportunity.

"Also," Jenna continued, "Christina lamented that she'd never get a promotion at Palmer Construction while Whitney was office manager, and she showed no signs of ever leaving. When Christina was hired,

Whitney had told her she was planning on opening her own realtor office, but last time Christina brought it up, Whitney laughed at her and called her crazy— why would she open her own office and carry all the overhead when she was getting to run her business for free from Palmer Construction?"

"I noticed when I was in Whitney's office to sign the contracts for The Dusty Attic that it was a real mess. Very disorganized."

"Which is strange because Whitney always struck me as being very organized," Jenna offered, and I nodded. Me too. At high school, she'd been on a couple of committees organizing various events and had been meticulous in her planning and delivery. She'd had notebooks color-coded with tags. Everything in its place. Her office had been at odds with what I remembered of her. My musings were cut short when Jenna nudged me and pointed out Bruce Sims and his dearly departed wife's best friend, Wendy Haley, standing together across the room.

"They look so sad," Jenna murmured. "I feel bad. We're all caught up in the excitement of finding Whitney's killer and forgetting that a woman died. Bruce's wife. Wendy's best friend. It must be awful for them."

"You have a good heart, Jenna Owens." Patting her arm, I added, "I'm going to say hello to them. You coming?"

"I'll catch up. Gotta use the facilities."

Leaving her in the bathroom, I weaved my way across the hall, stopping to speak to several people about the newly formed book club. I made a mental note to move on it quickly, while people were excited and interested. Hosting a book club at the store could be good for sales, and goodness knows I'd need them if I ever wanted to pay off my debt to Gran.

"Bruce. Wendy," I greeted. "How are you holding up?"

Wendy looked positively green, and I touched her arm in concern. "Are you all right? You don't look so good."

"I'm fine. It's a little warm in here, that's all."

"I'll get you a drink. That might help," Bruce offered.

I stopped him with a hand on his arm. "Steer clear of the eggnog unless you want the mother of all hangovers tomorrow."

He winked. "Your Gran been at it again?"

"Oh, good grief, she's infamous!"

"She's a character, that's for sure. Relax, I'll get water." He headed toward the buffet table.

"I just can't believe it," Wendy whispered, bottom lip trembling, eyes filling with tears. I didn't have to ask what she was referring to. She was clearly missing her best friend. Moving in close, I rubbed her back in what I hoped was a soothing gesture.

"I'm sorry for your loss." It seemed trite, but I didn't know what else to say. Wendy and Whitney had been inseparable at high school and it seemed they had remained close into adulthood.

"I saw her that morning. I'd baked more muffins. She used to tell me off, accuse me of sabotaging her diet, but I knew she secretly loved them. So, I kept baking. And I enjoy baking. It takes my mind off," she paused and swallowed, "things."

"What things?" I asked.

"Just stuff. Life. Work. You know."

"Right." I nodded. When I wanted to escape those things, I read a book. Wendy baked. Each to their own.

"She was just so—*alive*," Wendy continued, then laughed. "She was so nervous when she heard you'd moved back."

"Nervous? What on earth for?" Bruce had said something similar, and it had baffled me then, just like it did now.

"Because she'd always wanted to be like you. You were her measuring stick."

"I don't get it. She hated me. *Hated* me." I couldn't stress it enough. Whitney Sims had hated my guts. She'd told me to my face on more than one occasion. When I'd left Whitefall Cove, she'd told me it was the best thing that had ever happened to the town and that I wouldn't be missed. Oh, and to not hurry back.

"She wanted to be you. Or be like you. But

whenever she tried, it backfired. She tried to get her hair like yours and instead looked like she'd stuck her finger in an electric socket."

I put a hand to my hair, where it curled down past my shoulders. I'd left it loose tonight. Usually, I pulled it back into a simple ponytail, but I did nothing to my bland, brown tresses, nothing that would make Whitney envious.

"I'm sorry, but I'm having a hard time taking that in," I admitted. "Bruce said something similar to me and I just can't process it."

Wendy snorted. "Yeah, hard to believe, right? That was Whitney through and through. She projected this persona that wasn't the real her at all. She couldn't be content with her own life, couldn't be satisfied with what she had. There was a lot of envy. It was stressful for her."

"When the news hit that you'd had that meltdown in East Dondure, that your fiancé had cheated, and you'd zapped him with your magic, she was delighted. She'd been happy at your downfall. But then you got fired from your job and lost your witch's license, and you came home. Then she wasn't happy anymore. And when you put in the offer for The Dusty Attic and became her client? Her stress levels went through the roof," Wendy said.

I looked at the floor, imagining what that had been like for Whitney. "I knew none of that. I'm sorry if my coming back to Whitefall Cove made life difficult for her. I wish she were here now, so I could tell her that."

"Ha," Wendy barked, "she wouldn't have listened to you. She would have been snide and rude and, in her head, she'd have twisted it all around so that you were the bad guy. It's what she does. Did."

I was saved from responding by Bruce's return. He handed Wendy a bottle of water. "You've got more color now, feeling better?"

She nodded. "Yes, actually I am. Talking with Harper took my mind off it." Twisting the cap off, she took a sip. Bruce shrugged out of his jacket and tossed it over the back of a nearby chair.

"You're going to forget that later," Wendy pointed out.

"Probably," he agreed, scratching at his arm, "but I'm so darn itchy and the jacket was in the way."

"Want me to take a look?" Wendy offered, and I remembered she was a nurse.

Bruce shook his head. "Nah, it's all good, probably just a bite or something, but man, it sure itches." He was scratching as he talked, and I looked at the sleeve of his white button-down.

"Bruce?" I nodded at his arm. "You might want to take her up on that. You're bleeding."

A red stain was seeping through the cotton. "Darn," he cursed, fiddling with the cuff and rolling up his sleeve while Wendy grabbed his wrist and peered at the angry red rash on the inside of his forearm.

"Looks like an allergic reaction," she said.

My mind went straight to the borrio bud plant and what Jenna had told us. If you came into contact with it, it would cause a severe skin reaction. Could Bruce be the one who had stolen the plant? Did he kill his wife?

CHAPTER
NINE

"Everything okay here?" I turned to see Jackson approaching, his eyes intent on Bruce.

"Yeah, we're fine. Sorry to alarm you." Bruce shrugged, seeming unconcerned.

"We should probably go," Wendy added, "put something on that to take out the itch. Plus, people don't want to be seeing your arm oozing blood."

"Hang on a second." Jackson stopped them, grabbing Bruce's arm and examining the rash.

"What are you doing?" Bruce pulled his arm away, affronted.

Jackson planted his feet and stood with his fists on his hips, authority emanating from him in waves.

"What's going on?" Wendy asked, confused.

"Whitney was poisoned with a very rare toxic plant. One that was stolen from a greenhouse here in

Whitefall Cove recently. Sadly for the thief, they left behind a couple of leaves. Enough for us to trace—and identify—the plant."

"And I'm guessing you're going to tell me that you think my rash is associated with this plant?" Bruce asked, his tone resigned.

"I am," Jackson said. "The berries of this plant will kill you if ingested. But if you come into contact with the plant with your bare skin, you get a severe reaction. One that I'd imagine would look just like that." He nodded at Bruce's arm.

Bruce's face darkened, a flush of angry color in his cheeks, and his eyes narrowed as he glared at Jackson. "I did not kill my wife. I did not steal some toxic plant. I'm innocent."

"Then explain to me why you have this rash?" Jackson pressed.

"I don't know why," Bruce grumbled.

"It's an allergic reaction," Wendy cut in, her face deathly pale. "I'm a nurse," she added.

"What are you allergic to?" Jackson directed all of his attention to Bruce, who was now shifting from one foot to the other. I could practically see the cogs turning in Bruce's head. He knew this looked bad. He knew he was in trouble. He knew Jackson thought he was responsible for Whitney's death.

"Nothing." It was a quiet admission.

"Nothing that you know of," Wendy interrupted,

clutching at Bruce's free arm. "It doesn't mean he hasn't developed one, or come into contact with something new. A washing powder or soap can cause a reaction like this."

I looked at her, surprised by her level of anguish. Seemed Bruce was too, for he muttered, "Don't you say anything."

Jackson pounced, not missing a thing. "Say anything about what?" he demanded.

Wendy's eyes filled with tears and overflowed, running down her cheeks.

"Wendy. Don't," Bruce warned. She sniffed, trembling, her face so pale I feared she was about to pass out.

"I have to," she whispered. "People are going to find out soon enough, anyway."

"Curse it all," Bruce swore. Wrapping his arms around her, he pulled her to his chest where she clung to him. I watched with wide eyes. *Were they?*

"I'm pregnant," she sniffed, her voice barely above a whisper. "With Bruce's baby."

My jaw hit the floor and from Jackson's sudden stillness, I'm guessing the news took him by surprise, too.

"We're in love," she added, face buried in his chest. He looked at us over her head, his expression containing a gentleness I'd never seen in him before.

"It's true. Wendy and I have been having an affair," he said.

"How long has this been going on?" I cut in before Jackson had a chance to open his mouth. He cut me an angry glare, and I mouthed a sorry at him.

"Just over a year," Bruce said, wiping the tears from Wendy's cheeks with his thumbs and looking at her with such utter love and devotion on his face that my heart ached. Simon had never looked at me the way Bruce was looking at Wendy right now. This was what love looked like.

"But..." I looked from Bruce to Wendy and back again. "You're Whitney's best friend."

"I know!" she cried, distraught. "And I hated it. I hated I was doing this to her, but I just couldn't stop myself. I've *always* loved Bruce. Even when he married Whitney, I loved him. But I never acted on it. Never."

"Until a year ago," I pointed out, and she blushed.

"When he came to me, he was so desperately unhappy and we got to talking and we just clicked. One thing led to another."

"When he came to you?" I asked. "What did he come to you for?"

Bruce opened his mouth to warn her to shut up, but Wendy was on a roll and the words poured out. "Whitney knew her marriage was in trouble and decided that having a baby would fix it. Bruce came to me for help."

"Help, how?"

"He knows I'm a witch and a nurse. He wanted herbs or a spell to prevent Whitney from conceiving."

"Why didn't you just leave her?" I asked, stunned he'd go to such lengths. "If you were that unhappy? Why all the subterfuge? And then to have an affair on top of it?"

"I asked for a divorce before all of this." The pain etched in his voice was unmistakable. "But Whitney wouldn't hear of it. And she had a safety net. Maybe she knew this was coming before I did, maybe realized our marriage had died before I did—or before I finally did something about it. When I told her I wanted out, that our marriage was over, she revealed that she'd moved all of our assets into her name and that she'd take everything if I left her. Not only the house we lived in, but my investment portfolio as well. I'd be left with nothing."

"You believed her?"

"She showed me the deeds. She'd tricked me into signing documents and stupid me signed them without a second thought. Didn't even read them, didn't check. I can't believe I was such an idiot."

"What did you think you were signing?"

"Insurance papers. Whitney had gotten us a good deal on our insurance, so we were changing providers. She slipped the other papers in amongst the insurance documents, and I didn't even notice."

I looked at Jackson, who glanced my way. He shrugged and tilted his head sideways. Yeah, I nodded in agreement. Seemed Whitney was one crafty broad.

"You're going to have to come down to the station for questioning," Jackson said. "We'll take swabs of the arm for traces of the toxin from the borrio bud plant. Wendy, sorry, but you need to come too. I need you to make a statement repeating everything you've just told us." Bruce hung his head, his expression despondent.

Jackson led them out of the party, no one paying any attention as they gathered their coats and left. No one except for Christina, Mike, and Lexi, who all watched intently. Then they noticed me noticing and quickly disbanded. My mind was a whirl with the events that had just occurred and also a sense of disappointment that it was looking like Bruce had killed his wife after all. I'd been rooting for him to be innocent because I kinda liked the guy, but then I wasn't such a great judge of character. Simon had had me well and truly fooled.

My musing was disrupted by a commotion on the dance floor. Gran had conjured a stripper pole and was now happily gyrating around it in her massive green and red ball gown, the yards of tulle beneath the skirt flipping up to reveal red and white striped socks and bedazzled Ugg boots. Shaking my head on a laugh, I shuffled forward to watch the display, clapping along with everyone else as my grandmother made an absolute spectacle of herself. Life was never dull with her around, that was for sure.

"Isn't it exciting?" Slapping a plate piled high with pancakes in front of me, Gran snapped her wand and another batch of batter poured into the skillet. "Are you excited? I'm excited!"

"I can see that." I smiled, but it didn't reach my eyes.

"Harper Jones," she waggled a finger at me, "don't be a Debbie Downer. Today is exciting. The grand re-opening of The Dusty Attic."

"I'm just nervous." It was true, I was. Butterflies danced in my stomach and I felt nauseous. What if no one came? What if it was an unmitigated disaster?

"Stop being a drama queen and eat your food," Gran commanded in that don't-mess-with-me tone. I obeyed, shoving a forkful of pancake into my mouth.

Archie jumped up onto the chair next to me and head-butted my arm, giving me a mournful meow. "What?" I looked at him. "You've got food. Over there." I pointed with my fork. "In your dish." He responded by snaking out a paw, hooking a claw into my pancake and dragging it from my plate. Mission accomplished, he jumped down from the chair, taking the pancake with him, purring loudly.

"Thief!" I called after him. "Lucky I have plenty more or I wouldn't let you get away with that."

"Meow," he replied.

"I feel like I'm rushing it," I admitted to Gran. "Maybe I should wait till the new year."

"Are you brain impaired?" Gran leaned in close, checking my eyes. "The store is ready. So are you. It's not like you to be lacking confidence. It's all that Simon fella's fault. I'm gonna do that spell to make his wiener fall off."

I grabbed her wrist before she could rush off. "No, Gran. Don't. You're right. I didn't realize just how much the situation with Simon has affected me, making me question every little thing, always wondering if I'm making the wrong decision."

Her face softened, and she stroked my cheek. "When you're finished eating, I've laid out an outfit for you on your bed."

I couldn't contain my laughter. Gran jumped from one thing to another like a squirrel on steroids. It was exhausting keeping up with her, but I admitted that as nutty as she was, I was one hundred percent glad she was my family. I forced down another pancake, but nerves were making my stomach churn.

Pushing the plate away, I went upstairs to discover Gran had laid out a rather adorable red dress trimmed with white fur. My knee-high black boots would go perfectly with it. Very Christmassy. I'd been envisioning something gaudy and entirely inappropriate, but for once she'd pleasantly surprised me.

Changing into the dress, I spent extra time on my makeup and hair and was heading back downstairs when I heard her yell, "You ready yet?"

She stood by the front door with Archie at her heels. "What are you wearing?" I stopped mid-descent, shocked. She looked... normal. She was wearing a pair of navy pants, black court shoes, and a navy and white twin set. I'd never seen her in anything so understated in my entire life.

"Oh." She looked down at herself. "Don't you like it? I thought you would. I wanted to be normal for you today."

"Oh, Gran." I rushed the rest of the way down the stairs and hugged her. "Your normal is everyone else's crazy. I love your normal. Please don't change who you are because of me."

Her cheeky grin was back. "Well, in that case, I do have a backup outfit." With a flick of her wand, her outfit changed into garish parachute pants, a bright yellow sequined boob tube, a pink feather boa, topped off with a chunky, hand knitted cardigan that hung almost to her knees in a green and white snowflake pattern. This time her Ugg boots were bright blue.

"That's more like it." Kissing her cheek, I hooked my arm through hers and led the way to the car, Archie trotting along behind us.

When we arrived at The Dusty Attic, I was amazed to see a lineup of people waiting for the store to open. My heart leaped in my chest and a rush of adrenaline shot through me. Maybe my launch wasn't going to be a flop after all.

Gran high-fived everyone while I unlocked the door and flicked on the lights. It was freezing inside. Again. I rushed to the storeroom and flicked the thermostat back on. I had no idea why it kept turning off, but I really needed to do something about it. Customers wouldn't hang around if it was colder in my store than what it was outside.

"Gran, can you light the fire in the fireplace, please?" I whispered, taking up a position by the door, ready to greet my customers. A roaring open fire would warm the place up in no time.

While Gran lit the fire, I opened the door with a flourish. "Welcome to The Dusty Attic!" I beamed at the crowd.

A cheer rang out, and I felt the blood rush to my cheeks. I hadn't expected such a warm and enthusiastic welcome and I had to blink a couple of times to clear my vision. I shook everyone's hand as they filed into the store. Soon a fire was crackling, the coffee pot was on, and the store was full. Not as full as my heart, though. Archie had curled up into a ball on the rug in front of the fire. Several customers had snagged a book and were sitting in the armchairs, noses buried in the pages. This was exactly how I'd imagined it.

I'd just rung up another customer when Gran slid an arm around my waist. "It's going well, don't you think?" she asked.

"It's going brilliantly!" I smiled. "Thank you so much for your help, Gran. I couldn't have done this without you."

"Nonsense," she protested, but I saw the way her chest puffed out in pride.

By lunchtime, the crowd had thinned and my nerves were gone. I'd sold an amazing number of mystery books and almost every person in my store had asked about the book club, so much so that I knew I'd have to arrange it sooner rather than later. I'd overheard people speculating about Whitney and trying to guess where her body had been found and I realized that had been part of the attraction, but almost everybody had purchased something while nosing around, so I couldn't complain.

Jenna called by at lunchtime, bringing sandwiches with her.

"Thank you so much!" I said around a mouthful of ham, cheese, and pickle. "I'm starving."

"Thought you might be. Here's a tip as a small

business owner—don't forget to take breaks and stop to eat and drink, or you'll never last the day."

"If interest keeps up, I'll look at getting someone in part-time." Because what Jenna had said was true. Right now, I was starving, and I needed to pee. Both things were highly inconvenient while running a store on my own.

"I can help!" Gran piped up.

"Gran, you're so busy as it is, I don't want you to feel you have to come in here and work. You've done so much for me already." Slinging my arm around her shoulders, I hugged her to my side.

"You're right." She backtracked on her offer. "I'm not missing my pole dancing classes for anyone!"

Jenna poured us all a coffee and carried them over to my desk, where we were gathered. "So, have you heard?" she asked, glancing around, her voice low.

"Heard what?"

"That Bruce was released."

I'd filled both Jenna and Monica in on what had happened at the Christmas party last night, but hadn't had the chance to touch base with Jackson yet and find out anything new.

"No, I hadn't heard. There was a buzz in here this morning, but it was more around the fact that Whitney died here." Wrapping my hands around my coffee cup, I took a sip, sighing in delight. Delicious.

"Christina has been telling everyone that Bruce

and Wendy were arrested," Jenna murmured. "We need to have a meeting of our murder club."

I nodded. "Yes, we do. And they weren't arrested. Bruce was taken in for questioning and Wendy to give a statement. I don't think either of them was arrested."

"Yet," Gran said as if it were a done deal. "It's always the husband who did it."

I'd just locked up the store, Archie tucked under one arm, purse slung over my opposite shoulder, when I heard a man's voice calling my name. I turned to see Bruce Sims waving and hurrying down the sidewalk. I paused, waiting for him to reach me. It was dark and eerie, despite the early hour. I'd thought to keep my store open to cater to the after-work crowd and last-minute Christmas shoppers, but the streets were empty. Seemed late night shopping had yet to reach Whitefall Cove.

"Sorry," he called out, drawing closer. "Thanks for waiting."

"Not a problem," I called back. Archie meowed and wriggled in my arms, but I held tight. I didn't need him scampering off into the night. He'd get free rein once he was in the car. I'd already discovered he loved being in the car; traveling with him was no problem at all. And I also discovered that I enjoyed having him around. The customers did too. He got a lot of free pats and fusses today, and Gran had whipped up a litter tray, bowls, and food to keep at the store.

"Sorry, I need to take up jogging or something," Bruce puffed, reaching me. He bent over, hands on knees, while he fought to catch his breath.

"You're not alone there," I told him in sympathy. I badly needed to begin some sort of exercise regime if I didn't want to stack on the pounds living with Gran and her cooking.

Straightening, he gave me a lopsided smile.

"What can I do for you?" I asked.

"It's about Wendy." He twisted his hands, then slid them into his pockets and rocked back on his heels. "I'm worried about her. All of this stress isn't good for her. Or the baby."

"No, I imagine not," I agreed, "but I can't see what that has to do with me."

"Oh no, I didn't mean it was your fault," he protested, "not at all. This mess is of our own making, but well... now the town knows." He shrugged. "She's been struggling with morning sickness as it is, and then Whitney dying the way she did. Despite everything, Whitney was her friend and I know she misses her terribly."

"Did the two of you have a plan?" I asked, beyond

curious about what they thought would have happened, "because Wendy's pregnancy wouldn't have stayed a secret for long. Were you intending to tell Whitney? About Wendy and the baby? Or keep your involvement out of it?"

"We were, yes." He nodded emphatically. "We'd decided we were going to tell her before Wendy even got pregnant. I wanted to do it six months ago, but Wendy wanted me to at least try to get some of my assets back."

"And did you?"

"Sort of. I discovered one investment property that hadn't been switched over. Whitney must have missed it. That was going to be our nest egg to rebuild. Whitney could think she had the rest, but I was going to fight her for it in court. And then Wendy got pregnant, and it was iffy there at the beginning and I didn't want her to have the extra stress of the blowup that was bound to happen with Whitney and the townsfolk gossiping."

He puffed out his cheeks and looked sheepish. "And now look at the big rotten mess we're in. I know it looks bad for me, but I swear I didn't kill Whitney. Yes, I wanted her out of my life, but I wasn't prepared to risk going to jail for it. I've got plans. With Wendy. Being sent away for murder is not one of them."

I was thinking that Whitney's death had worked in Bruce's favor. Their combined assets were now all his.

But as he said, he wanted to be with Wendy. He wouldn't risk being sent to jail, to be kept away from her and their baby.

I lapsed into silence, pondering it all. A car roaring past shattered the quiet. A loud popping noise had me turning my head, thinking the car had backfired, when Bruce shouted, "Get down!" and dived at me. We went down in a tangle of limbs, Archie clutched to my chest. My head hit the sidewalk with a crack, and I lay there dazed, looking up at the night sky. Bruce groaned and rolled off me.

"Are you okay?" I asked, shocked at what had just happened, and winded by the fall and weight of him. Archie meowed in protest and I ran my fingers over his fur, checking he wasn't hurt but refusing to let him go.

Bruce groaned. "Think I'm hit. Hurts like the devil."

I sat up. "What?" Sure enough, in the light from the street lamp, I could see a smear of blood on the sidewalk and Bruce clutching his thigh. Blood oozed between his fingers. With shaking hands, I dug around in my purse for my phone and dialed.

"Hey, Harper," Jackson answered on the second ring.

"I'm with Bruce Sims outside my store," I said, my voice shaking. "He's been shot."

I heard a clatter, then Jackson saying, "Where was he shot?"

"Outside my store."

"No, Harper," he said with exaggerated patience, "where on his body? Is he alive?"

"Oh." I could feel my face heat at my idiocy. "He's alive, yes. He was shot in the leg. A car drove by. I didn't pay any attention to it and then a popping sound—gunshots—and Bruce dove at me and told me to get down. Or possibly the other way around. He yelled to get down and then pushed me to the ground. But most likely it happened simultaneously." I was rambling but couldn't stop my runaway mouth.

"Paramedics are on their way," Jackson reported, multitasking behind the scenes. "Are you hurt?"

Despite a throbbing on the back of my head where I'd whacked it on the sidewalk, I was not hurt. "I'm fine." My voice wobbled, and I prayed he didn't notice, or if he did, he'd ignore it.

"I'm on my way. If you can, apply pressure to the wound."

"Okay." I disconnected the call and dropped my phone back into my purse. Whipping off my coat belt, I wrapped it around Bruce's leg as a makeshift bandage, then placed both hands on the top and applied pressure as instructed. I'd had to release Archie, and I kept one eye on him worried he might wander out onto the road and get hit by a car. As if sensing my mounting distress, he moved to the doorstep of the store and sat, watching us with his big golden eyes.

"How are you doing?" I asked Bruce, trying to sound brave, but my hands shook as I pressed them to his wound, trying to stem the bleeding. The belt wasn't doing much good.

"I'm fine," he lied, his face bathed in sweat. "You know, if she weren't already dead, this is the type of stunt I'd expect Whitney to pull."

"But who would want to kill you, Bruce?" Because this threw a spanner in the works. I'd been leaning toward him being guilty, despite all his protests, although I actually thought he was quite a nice guy. He and Wendy had so much motive to want Whitney out of the way, it wasn't too much of a leap to think he'd killed her.

A car with a flashing blue light lodged on the dashboard screeched to a halt at the curb. "Hi, Jackson." My voice wavered, and I cleared my throat, trying not to show how utterly freaked out I was. He crossed the sidewalk in two big strides and crouched by my side, scowling when he saw the stain on my dress.

"It's not my blood," I told him. I knew it wasn't mine because I'd freaked out when I first saw it too, until I realized Bruce had bled all over me when he landed on me.

"What happened?" Jackson directed the question

to Bruce as he examined his wound, removing my ineffectual belt. "No arterial bleed," he murmured, more to himself than us. "Through and through."

"Dark sedan. Couldn't see the driver," Bruce grunted. "Partial plate though. BC1."

Jackson pulled out his phone and typed in what Bruce had told him. I hadn't even thought to get the car's license plate. All I knew was that it had four wheels and an engine and that was only because I heard the latter.

The ambulance arrived, pulling in behind Jackson's car, and two paramedics climbed out. One examined Bruce while the other turned to me, but I shooed him away. "I'm fine, seriously. He's the one who's been shot."

"She hit her head," Bruce told them. "It made a hell of a crack when we went down."

Jackson's head snapped toward me. "You didn't tell me that."

I shrugged. "It's not important. I'm fine, seriously, a little headache is all." The paramedic shone a light in my eyes, then felt around my scalp. When his fingers pressed on the swelling egg beneath my hairline, I couldn't hide the wince.

"We'll take you to the hospital as a precaution," he told me. "Maybe a scan to make sure you don't have a brain bleed."

"What?" Jackson and I said in unison.

Then I regained my senses. "No. I don't want to go to the hospital. I told you, I'm fine."

"Will you just let them take care of you?" Jackson ran his fingers through his hair and stood over me, doing a wonderful impression of an intimidating cop. I was sufficiently intimidated.

"I can't leave Archie here by himself, wandering the streets. And I somehow doubt they'll let me take him with me to the hospital." I nodded toward my ginger cat who was now grooming himself and, apparently, disinterested in the excitement happening mere feet away.

Jackson scooped Archie up into his arms with zero protests from my cat. Carrying him to his car, he deposited him onto the passenger seat before returning. "He'll be safe there. Once I've finished here, I'll take him to your Gran's."

"When you're finished here? What do you mean?" I asked, watching as Bruce was strapped to a stretcher and wheeled toward the ambulance.

"I need to find the bullet," Jackson said, shining his torch around the garden bed directly in front of The Dusty Attic windows.

"Isn't it in Bruce's leg?" I frowned, confused.

"It went all the way through," Jackson explained, "meaning what's left of it should be here somewhere. It's evidence."

I nodded. "Right." No wonder the bleeding hadn't stopped. I was only plugging one hole. I shuddered.

"Your turn." The paramedics had returned.

"I'm not getting on a stretcher," I said, reluctantly following them to the unit.

"No need. You can ride up front with me. Stu needs to ride in the back with the patient, anyway."

"Oh well, in that case, fine." I paused at the passenger door and turned back to Jackson. "Please take care of Archie." The wobble was back in my voice and I clutched my purse to my chest, trying to hide my trembling.

Jackson paused his bullet search and looked directly at me, his eyes boring into me as if he could see my soul. "I will guard him with my life. No harm will come to him while in my care," he promised. I nodded. *Right, that's good then.*

The paramedic helped me up into the cab. I'd already forgotten his name.

"You all right there, Harper?" Bruce asked from the rear of the unit, his voice thick and heavy.

"Yeah. I'm okay," I said. "How about you?"

"They've got some good drugs."

"Care to share?" I twisted to see him sucking on a green whistle-type contraption.

"Nothing for you. You have a head injury," the paramedic told me. Then we were off to the hospital.

"You appear to attract trouble." Officer Miles stood at the foot of the gurney I was sitting on, her face a mask of impatience.

"A natural talent." I shrugged. I'd received the all clear, been given a couple of painkillers for my headache, and told to report back immediately if I experienced any other symptoms. "You here to question Bruce?" I asked, digging in my purse for my phone. I'd call Jenna or Monica to come to pick me up.

"Bruce is in surgery. I'm here to take you home."

"Sure you are." I snorted, not believing her.

She crossed her arms, her face deadpan. "I am."

"You are?"

She sighed. "If it weren't for the fact that you've sustained a head injury..." I figured she'd been about to say something insulting before she stopped herself. I guess I should be grateful for small mercies. "They told me you're free to leave, so come on, let's go." She went to take my purse from me, but I snatched it to my chest as if she were a bag thief. She held both hands up. "Fine."

Easing off the edge of the gurney, I slid my purse onto my shoulder and straightened my coat. I'd lost the belt. Goodness knows where it had ended up, but it didn't matter. It would be covered in blood now, anyway. I followed Officer Miles out of emergency to the squad car parked outside.

"Is The Dusty Attic a crime scene again?" I asked, breaking the frosty silence.

"Detective Ward has called forensics in tonight," she replied, slamming her door and gunning the engine, keeping her eyes facing front.

She was infuriating. I didn't know what that meant. Would I have access to my bookstore or not? "Can I open in the morning?" I tried a more direct question.

"Affirmative," was the clipped response.

"Good." Trying to make conversation with Officer Miles was like trying to get Monica to sunbathe. Never going to happen. Instead, I let the silence surround me, watching out the window as the streetlights whizzed past. Within minutes, we were in front of Gran's house. I climbed out, said thank you, and slammed the door. She drove off immediately, and I stood watching the patrol car's taillights disappear down the road.

"We need to call a meeting of the murder club!" Gran said from the doorway, waving at me to come inside.

"Is Archie here?" I asked, hurrying up the path. Archie meowed in greeting, pushing past Gran's legs to welcome me. "Oh, there you are. You okay, boy?"

Picking him up, I buried my face in his fur and promptly burst into tears.

"Long day, sweetheart?" Gran put an arm around my shoulders and ushered me inside. "But you're okay or the docs wouldn't have let you out."

"I'm fine." I sniffed, wiping my face. "It was just all so... shocking!"

"Come inside and tell me all about it. I've got a brandy with your name on it."

"I don't think I'm meant to drink alcohol with a head injury," I pointed out.

"Push smoosh." She waved away my concerns. "How about a soothing cup of tea, then?"

I stopped and looked at her. "Who are you and what have you done with my Gran?"

CHAPTER
ELEVEN

It was a busy morning at The Dusty Attic. Gran came in to lend a hand, even though I'd reassured her I was fine. My headache was gone, as was the lump on the back of my skull, and a good night's sleep had done me the world of good. I'd woken this morning with Archie curled against my side, his warm body comforting, and I felt more my usual self and not the crying wreck of the night before.

I came into work expecting crime scene tape outside, but there was nothing to indicate anything had occurred except for the bloodstain on the sidewalk. Gran took care of it with a wave of her wand and I left her to serve customers while I called a local maintenance man to come and check the thermostat, which was in the off position again this morning. That meant another chilly start. Burt Reynolds—seriously, that was his name—assured me he would drop in today to take a look. He wondered if it was on some sort of timer that I didn't know about since the store had sat empty for so long.

I'd just hung up from speaking with Burt when my phone rang again.

"Harper Jones," I answered, eyeballing the boxes of books in the storeroom and making a mental note that I needed to sort through them and also to set up some vendor accounts with printers and publishers—if books continued to fly off the shelves, I'd need to restock sooner rather than later.

"Hi, Harper, this is Amy from Mr. Sims's office at the Whitefall Cove Bank."

"Oh, hi, Amy, what can I do for you?"

"I was just clearing Mr. Sims's desk since he'll be out on leave for a while and I noticed he'd put a note on your file to ask you to drop in a copy of your purchase contract for The Dusty Attic. It's not urgent. We just need a copy for our records."

"Sure, that's not a problem at all..." I paused, trying to remember where I'd put the contract. "Oh. Uh, I'm not sure I have a copy," I admitted. "I signed it with Whitney the morning she died. I don't recall getting a copy." The truth was, I hadn't given it any thought. I'd left Whitney's office without the keys to the bookstore and assumed she'd give me my copy of the contract when we met later to hand over the keys. Only that never happened. The police initially had possession of the keys until Jackson had given them back to me so I could research what had killed Whitney. I wondered if they had the contract too? Maybe it had been in Whitney's purse and was now evidence.

"Well, if you could follow up with Palmer Construction, perhaps? It's most likely in her office."

"Yes, you're right. I'll chase that up and get a copy for you as soon as possible."

"No rush, just something we need on hand for the auditors."

"Okay. Thanks for the call, Amy. I'll drop in a copy when I have it."

After hanging up, I went out to speak with Gran, who was flirting outrageously with a young man who was flirting back with equal fervor. Once he left, I asked, "Gran, have you seen a copy of the purchase contract for this place lying around anywhere? I don't remember Whitney giving me my copy, but a lot happened that day and maybe I put it down at home or something."

Gran readjusted her bra while she considered my question. "Nope, can't say I have. Why?"

"Oh, the bank wants a copy to keep on file."

"You can probably get a copy from Mike," Gran pointed out.

I nodded. "Yeah, that's what Amy said. Do you mind holding down the fort while I pop over and see?"

"Sure, love, I've got this all under control."

Palmer Construction was within walking distance, not on Main Street where Jenna and I worked, but the street running across the end of Main, not quite on the corner but just visible from the *Tribune* offices. I decided to duck in to see Jenna on the way past, fill her in on what had happened the night before. Her office was upstairs and wasn't so much an office as an open workspace she shared with three others. Jenna had pushed her desk over to the window, so she could monitor the comings and goings of Main Street. I called it spying, but Jenna insisted she was doing a community service.

"Good morning." I came up behind her, making her jump.

Hand on her chest, she spun in her chair. "Jeez, Harper, little early in the morning for scaring the bejesus out of me, don't you think?" She grumbled, then frowned. "Why aren't you at The Dusty Attic?"

"Don't fret." I leaned on the edge of her desk. "Gran's there taking care of things. I just need to pop into Whitney's office and see if she has my contract. The bank wants a copy and I don't recall her giving me the final signed copy."

"Right," Jenna said, took a mouthful of coffee and grimaced. "Yuk. Cold." She put the cup back down in disgust. "So, you just popped in to say hello on your way past?"

"Actually, no." I leaned down and lowered my voice, telling her about the shooting last night.

"Harper, are you okay?" she whispered, grabbing my wrist, then glancing around to make sure her co-workers weren't watching.

"I'm fine," I reassured her, "but Bruce got a partial license plate. And I was thinking with your research skills and informants, maybe..." I trailed off.

"You're thinking I could find out who the car belongs to?" she finished. She unearthed a notepad on her desk and grabbed a pencil. "Give it to me."

"B-C-1," I told her. "It's a dark sedan."

She tucked the pencil behind her ear. "Leave it with me. I know someone who might help. And don't ask. I can't reveal my sources."

I nodded, then slapped her on the shoulder as I straightened. "FYI, Bruce is still in the hospital—if you wanted to get some photos to go with your breaking story?" I winked. Maybe this would get her editor off her back for not breaking Whitney's murder case. She scooped up her phone and followed me downstairs, intent on getting the story before any of her co-workers. I bid farewell to her out the front and continued on to Palmer Construction.

A feeling of déjà vu swept over me as I pushed open the door to their offices. It was the same, but different. Christina sat at her desk, busy with a pile of paperwork. Mike had just stepped out of his office, coffee in hand, when he spied me.

"Good morning, Harper." He smiled. "Didn't expect to see you today. How are things? How's the store?"

I didn't know if anyone at Palmer Construction knew about Bruce yet, that he'd been shot, but I decided they weren't going to hear it from me because I'd been thinking about it ever since it had happened. Someone wanted Bruce dead. They'd tried to kill him. Which meant there was a fair chance that same person killed Whitney. The question was, why? I really wanted to talk with Jackson about the whole thing and had plans to visit him at the police station once I'd finished here.

"Things are going very well, thank you." I smiled in return, allowing Mike to usher me into his office. He closed the door and indicated the seat in front of his desk.

"What can I do for you?" he asked.

"I got a call from the bank. They need a copy of my contract for the bookstore and I realize with everything that happened that day, Whitney didn't actually give me my copy. I was wondering if it was here. In her office."

He sighed, pinching the bridge of his nose. "Most likely. Sorry about that. I don't like to speak ill of the dead, but Whitney was dropping the ball on a lot of things lately."

I wondered if Whitney had suspected her husband of having an affair. That would explain her distraction and lack of attention to detail.

Mike stood and opened his office door. "Christina!" he called. "Can you please check in Whitney's office for Harper's contract of sale?"

"Absolutely not," Christina snapped. "You want me to find it? You pay me her salary."

"You have got to be kidding me." Mike groaned, banging his head softly against the doorframe.

Alarmed, I stood and touched his arm. "Hey, it's okay. Would you mind if I looked? I know things were tense between Christina and Whitney and clearly, Christina is still very angry, so..."

"Be my guest." He sounded weary, beaten down, and I decided to hold off asking about the bonus he'd paid Whitney now that I had the opportunity to poke around in her office. Something I hadn't expected.

I followed Mike to Whitney's office, where he flung open the door. It was clear the police had been here. Fingerprint powder covered her desk and the papers and files that had been strewn about were now neatly stacked in a box. Another box sat on the floor.

"Might take you a while," Mike apologized. "The police didn't take any of her paperwork as far as I'm aware. It's been boxed up though, so you may have to dig." He shook his head as he closed the door behind him, leaving me alone.

Starting at the box on her desk, I began sifting through the piles of papers and files, searching for my contract but also keeping my eyes peeled for anything of interest. What if my earlier thoughts were correct and whoever killed Whitney had taken a shot at Bruce? That meant the killer was still out there—and it wasn't Bruce. I texted Jenna and Monica.

Murder Club meeting at The Dusty Attic, tonight at eight.

I'm in, Jenna wrote back immediately. Nothing from Monica, but since she worked nights, I figured she'd read my message later and get back to me then.

I went through everything in the box, laying it out into relevant piles. Client files on the left, correspondence on the right. Like it or not, Mike was going to have to hire someone—or pay Christina extra —to sort out the whole mess, and while I was more than capable of doing it, I now had my own business to run, plus I didn't want to overstep the mark. A little voice in my head reminded me I was massively overstepping by snooping through Whitney's office in the first place.

And then I found it. Not only my contract, but also a black-and-white photograph, printed on standard office paper, of Mike in a passionate embrace with a woman. It was stuck between two pieces of paper and

I assumed the police had flicked through Whitney's paperwork so fast the photo had been missed. Sliding the picture into my purse, I picked up the contract and let myself out, waving the contract at Christina who quickly slammed shut a file on her desk when I appeared. "Found it!" I called.

"Great," she muttered, obviously not caring.

"Thank Mike for me, would you? Bye."

"Bye." I could feel her eyes bore into my back as I walked out.

"I hereby call the murder club to order!" Gran announced with a flourish. Jenna and Monica smiled indulgently while I shook my head in resignation. Monica had brought pizza, and we were seated in front of the fireplace at The Dusty Attic, eating.

"I hope you're not telling people that we have a murder club," I muttered, wiping my hands on a napkin.

"Of course not." Settling back into an armchair, Gran patted her lap and Archie immediately jumped up, kneaded her thighs into submission before curling up in a ball, his purr showing his contentment. "So, we going to get started or what?"

Moving the bookcase out of the way, I revealed the crime board. Monica jumped up and began updating the timeline with what we'd learned about Bruce and Wendy.

"Here's what you don't know," I said to Monica. "Last night, someone tried to kill Bruce."

"What?" Monica blinked, her mouth dropping open. I looked at Gran, shocked. I thought she would have blabbed the first chance she got, but she'd proved me wrong.

"Don't look at me like that," Gran grumbled. "I didn't tell anyone what happened here last night. I don't think I've ever seen you so upset, not even with all the trouble with Simon McDouche-face."

"Here? It happened here?" Monica gasped, eyes stricken as she turned to me.

I nodded. "I was locking up. Bruce was coming down the street and called out for me to wait, so I did. We were talking when a car went past and opened fire. He got hit. He's okay; the bullet hit his leg."

"Geez." Monica shook her head. "A drive-by shooting in sleepy little Whitefall Cove."

"What do the police think?" Gran asked, and I shrugged.

"Jackson was here last night, searching for the bullet. I haven't talked to him since then."

"What do *you* think? This changes things, doesn't it? That maybe he didn't kill Whitney? Or do we have two killers on the loose?" Monica asked.

"That's why I wanted to meet," I said. "To sort

through all that we know. And there's something else."

"There's more?" Monica resumed her seat on the sofa, arching a brow. I taped the photo of Mike and the woman he was kissing up on the board. Monica and Jenna peered at it.

"That's definitely Mike Palmer," Jenna said. "And the woman? That looks like it could be Lexi."

"Lexi? The barista from Bean Me Up?" I asked, peering at the grainy image.

"Could be," Monica murmured. "Couldn't be one hundred percent sure, though. But the height and build fit. With the angle of her head, it's hard to say for sure."

"I found this in Whitney's office. I'm wondering if she was blackmailing Mike. It could explain the out-of-character Christmas bonus," I said.

"Oh my goodness, you think?" Jenna clutched her hand to her chest. "That's just awful! And so typical Whitney."

"It is, but I don't understand why. What's so terrible about him kissing Lexi—assuming it's her?" I asked.

"The age difference?" Jenna guessed. "Mike has to be in his forties, yeah? And Lexi is what? Early twenties?"

"But would you pay ten grand to keep that quiet? A little scandalous, sure, but who would really care?"

"I think I know why," Monica piped up. "Mike is a wolf shifter. Lexi is a fox shifter."

"So what?" I asked. "What does that matter?"

"The foxes and wolves have been feuding in Whitefall Cove for generations. This would be big. And bad. I'd understand Mike not wanting to get found out."

"What do we think happened?" I asked. "Whitney suspected something was up, followed Mike and snapped this photo, then used it to blackmail him? But Mike paid the blackmail, so why kill her? If he was intending to kill her to keep her quiet, surely he wouldn't have paid the blackmail demand in the first place?"

"You're all assuming it was blackmail," Gran piped up. "You don't have any hard evidence of that. You should get some."

"How though? It's not like we can just ask Mike about it," Monica argued.

"Why can't we?" Jenna responded. "Sometimes you get the answers you need if you tackle the issue head-on."

Our discussion was interrupted by a banging on the door. We all looked at each other, then at Gran. "Did you invite someone else?" I wouldn't put it past her. Gran was notoriously bad at keeping secrets. She could have let slip to anyone that we were meeting here tonight.

"I already told you I haven't breathed a word." She mimed zipping her lips, and I sighed.

Well, someone was here, making an unholy racket. Crossing to the door, I pulled up the blind to see Jackson standing on the other side, fist raised to bang again. He paused, arm in the air, when he saw me. Quickly unlocking the door, I ushered him inside.

"Jackson! What are you doing here?" I completely forgot that our crime board was on display.

He didn't miss a thing, his eyes zeroing in on it over my shoulder. He brushed past me as he spoke. "Saw the light on, thought I'd check in. What's this?"

"Oh, that's..." I shrugged. It was blatantly obvious what it was, and I shot a weak smile in his direction.

"You ladies aren't doing what I think you're doing, are you?" He turned to face us, arms crossed, face dark. "This is serious business. Police business. You stick your noses in where they're not wanted, and you might find yourselves a target."

Gran audibly swallowed, but I suspected she did it for dramatic effect. She wasn't intimidated by anyone, let alone a murderer.

"Yes, but listen." I crossed to the board and pointed to the timeline. "We all thought Bruce did it, right? I mean, obviously. He's been having an affair with his wife's best friend, gets her pregnant. Wife is already threatening to take every last penny—he's trapped between a rock and a hard place. It makes sense that his only option is to get rid of the wife."

Jackson inclined his head and grumbled, "Continue."

"What if someone else knew all that? Knew about Bruce's affair and staged the murder to implicate him?"

"Also possible, but then why shoot him? Their plan would have been that he go to jail. If they wanted him dead, why not poison him along with Whitney?"

"Good point," Monica purred, her eyes devouring Jackson.

"Then there's the ten-thousand-dollar bonus that Mike paid Whitney." I changed tack. "I found this photo amongst the paperwork on Whitney's desk. What if she was blackmailing Mike?"

Jackson plucked the photo from the board and inspected it. "Is this Lexi?" he asked no one in particular.

"We think so," I said.

"You're suggesting that Mike would pay a sizeable sum of money to keep his tryst with Lexi secret?"

"It's a possibility," I argued defensively, taking the photo from him and sticking it back on the board. "Monica was telling us that Lexi is a fox shifter and Mike a wolf shifter, and apparently the two clans have been feuding for years."

"Interesting." Jackson crossed to the pizza box on

the coffee table and snagged himself a slice. "You haven't finished your timeline though," he pointed out.

"Maybe you can help?" Monica glided up to me and took the marker from my hand. I took her place on the sofa, letting her take the lead.

"Maybe," he said.

"So, here's what we don't know," she said and tapped the timeline. "What time Whitney started her day and what she ate or drank before she met with Harper at nine. We know Christina brought takeout coffee for everyone. Whitney didn't drink hers in front of Harper, so maybe she didn't have one. We know Wendy dropped in home-baked muffins. Did Whitney eat one? We also don't know Whitney's movements between when Harper left her office to when she came here to The Dusty Attic."

"So, you don't know how the poison was administered," Jackson summarized.

"Exactly!"

Jackson remained silent, studying the board and chewing. We waited. When he'd finished his pizza slice, he dusted his hands together and turned to us. "I'm impressed. For amateurs, you've done okay. I'll strike a deal with you."

"Oh?"

"I'll help you fill in the blanks, since I get the overwhelming sense that you will not let this go." He was looking right at me when he said it. I bit my lip but didn't answer, waiting for him to continue. "In exchange, you tell me immediately when you get any new information. And you don't breathe a word of this to anyone. I'm taking a chance, and if it looks like you lot are going to damage my career, I'll shut you down. Got it?"

"Got it," we chorused, faces alight with excitement.

"Why? Why are you letting us help?" The words were out of my mouth before I could stop them, but I had a burning curiosity about why he'd decided not to shut us down.

"Because you can be of help to me. I'd rather work with you than be worrying you're all about to get yourselves killed. You find any clues, you tell me. You have a theory, you tell me. You do not go accusing anyone of anything, got it?" We nodded. "Plus, people open up to you, Harper. I've seen it in action. I'm used to people lying to me, or not talking at all. It comes with the job, but with you? They're more likely to let slip a vital detail."

"That I can then pass on to you," I said flatly, not sure why I suddenly felt deflated. He was using us to solve this case. I didn't know why that bothered me, but it did.

CHAPTER
TWELVE

"I don't see why you've got your panties in a wad," Gran protested at home later that night. "He basically said you scratch my back, I'll scratch yours."

"I know." I sighed.

"You're using him too, you know," she pointed out. "He filled in some of the missing blanks on your timeline, didn't he? He told you the poison was in the coffee, that Whitney hadn't eaten breakfast, that the muffins were tested and came up clean. He gave you a lot, actually."

"I know," I repeated.

"It's because you have the hots for him." Gran nodded, waving her wand over the stove where she was preparing a late supper. She hadn't eaten much of

159

the pizza, complaining it gave her heartburn. Now she was whipping up a batch of macaroni and cheese.

"What?" I protested. "I do not!"

She snorted. "Lie all you like to yourself, but you can't lie to me. You don't get to my age without picking up a few things—and the mutual attraction between two people is one of those things that I never miss," she assured me. "The problem is," she continued on, ignoring my horrified expression, "he's seeing someone else. And given your recent experience with Simon McDouche-face, the very idea of getting involved with a taken man is reprehensible to you."

"I didn't know you knew such big words," I grumbled, deflecting.

"Sassy," she laughed. "But you know I'm right and that is a burr under your saddle that is irritating your lily-white hide."

"Well, there's a pleasant visual." I didn't want to discuss Detective Jackson Ward anymore; didn't want to think of him in the romantic sense, because what Gran said was true. He was off limits. Taken. I would not daydream about an unavailable man. Archie saved the day by trotting in and dropping a live mouse at my feet. I screamed, scrambling back as the rodent scampered toward my foot.

"Archie!"

"It's just a mouse. Harmless." Gran laughed at me as I climbed onto the chair. I hated mice. And spiders.

And snakes. In fact, I had a healthy list of critters that I'd prefer very much if my cat did not bring into the house. "Wait." I pinned a glare on Gran. "How did he catch a mouse?"

"The usual way I'd imagine." Gran shrugged, spooning up a plate of macaroni and cheese. She carried it over to the table and placed it in front of me, uncaring that I was crouched on my chair.

"But... wasn't the mouse... outside?"

"I would think so," she nodded, plating up her own serving of food.

"So how did Archie get outside? And then back in again? With a mouse?"

She shot me a look. "Through the cat door, of course." Shaking her head as if she thought I was the biggest imbecile on earth, Gran seated herself and shoveled in big mouthfuls of macaroni. She really must have been hungry.

"Since when do we have a cat door?"

"Since today, when Archie asked for one."

"Archie asked? He's a cat. He can't talk," I pointed out.

"He's a familiar and he most certainly can," she shot back. Eyes round and mouth hanging open, I gaped at her. My cat could speak? Why didn't he speak to me?

"Because you're not ready," Gran answered, even though I hadn't asked out loud. "Plus, you don't have your magic. It would take more effort on his behalf for you to hear and understand him, so he mentioned to me that a cat door would be most welcome."

"Oh." I had no words. I'd let my connection to the world of magic and witches slide when I was in the city. Instead, I'd focused on my career and now I felt out of touch, out of the loop. I wasn't aware that familiars could have such a close relationship with their witches that they could communicate in such a manner.

"And that is why you're attending classes at Drixworths." Gran pointed her fork at me.

"Please stop reading my mind," I whispered. "It's really disconcerting." I saw the mouse head under the refrigerator out of the corner of my eye. "Can you please remove the mouse?"

She absently waved her wand. "Done. Just know that he brought it in as a gift for you."

"He did?" Now I felt awful. Archie had brought me a gift, and I'd carried on like it was the worst thing in the world. Lowering my butt onto my chair, I stared down at my orange cat who sat looking up at me, his golden eyes sad. "Oh, I'm sorry, Archie." I bent and picked him up, cuddling him to my chest. "I appreciate the thought, I really do, but please, no live little critters, okay?" He meowed in response and head-butted my chin, which I took as a sign of forgiveness. Putting him on the chair next to me, I pulled my bowl of macaroni closer and ate, closing my eyes in bliss. If I kept eating like this, I was going to get fat, but right now I didn't care.

When we'd finished, Gran cleaned up the kitchen with her magic, making me wish yet again that I had my own powers back. I hadn't thought I'd miss it as much as I did, but now I felt reliant on Gran and it was another thing that didn't sit well with me. I knew she knew what I was thinking, for I caught her speculative look, but she didn't say anything, just announced she was going to bed.

"Goodnight, I'll be up later. I've got some paperwork for the store to get through," I said.

"Don't stay up too late." Then she was gone, leaving me at the kitchen table with nothing but the sound of the ticking clock on the wall to break the silence. And Archie's snoring. He'd curled into a ball on the chair next to me and was now sound asleep.

Pulling out my contract for The Dusty Attic, I smoothed the dog-eared pages and placed it on the table. Of course, I'd read it before signing, but now I went through it again at a more leisurely pace. It wasn't until I got to the appendix pinned to the back that I thought something was amiss. The valuation of the store was higher than what I'd paid. How could that be? I mean, yay for me, but surely that wasn't right? Maybe a typo? Stifling a yawn, I decided I'd ask Bruce tomorrow. I wasn't a numbers person; I was a words person and maybe I was reading it all wrong.

Both Jenna and Monica met me for lunch at Bean Me Up. Monica was buried beneath a wide-brimmed hat, shades, and a turned-up coat. Sunlight won't kill a vampire, but it can give them a nasty burn, which was why most of them only came out at night. But today was Monica's day off and occasionally she liked to mingle with the day folk.

"How's business?" Jenna asked, perusing the menu.

"Fantastic, but I have to assume that sales are this good because of my re-opening and it being three days before Christmas."

Jenna nodded. "Yeah, you'll probably experience a New Year slump. Although the town is definitely abuzz with your return, so you have that in your favor."

"Maybe I need to start a business," Monica mused, tossing her menu onto the table. "I feel left out. I'm just an employee. I turn up, do my job, and go home. Oh, and they pay me." She grinned.

"Er, hello, I'm an employee too. But you could always start your own bar or club," Jenna suggested. "Your cocktails are amazing."

"I don't know if I want the bother. All the overhead

and stress. Weren't you just saying yesterday that you'd forgotten to arrange insurance for The Dusty Attic, Harper?"

"What?" Jenna gasped. "Harper! That's not like you."

I looked sheepish. "I know, I know. It was my bookkeeper who picked up on it. As Monica said, I'm used to being an employee. Having all these extra responsibilities is new to me."

"What ended up happening with Burt Reynolds? Did he fix the thermostat?" Jenna asked. She'd referred Burt to me.

"He says he can't find anything wrong," I grumbled. Every morning since taking ownership, the thermostat had been off, despite it being left on the previous night. He'd searched for a timer and checked the wiring. Despite finding nothing wrong, he'd offered to change the thermostat control box, guessing that it possibly had an undetected fault in it.

"Boo," Monica sympathized. "That sucks."

"Oh, and get this." I leaned forward, and they mirrored my action. "I found something weird with the numbers in my contract last night."

"Weird how?" Monica asked.

"Well, not so much the contract, but the appendix. The valuation is way higher than what I paid."

"A clerical error?" Jenna suggested.

"I went to visit Bruce this morning and asked him to take a look."

"He's out of hospital then?"

"Yeah, recuperating at Wendy's place. And she's a nurse, so..." I shrugged. Bruce was in expert hands.

"What did he say? About the contract?" Monica cut in, impatient to hear the answer.

"The contract was correct; the appendix was wrong. He suggested maybe Whitney was smudging the figures."

"Why? What would be the point of that?"

"Because the insurance company uses the figures from the appendix. It has the valuation of the property and that's what they base their premiums on."

"So, she changes the figures to show a higher valuation, meaning you pay a higher premium for your insurance?"

"Exactly!"

"But she must benefit somehow," Monica pointed out. "Otherwise, why do it? Just to screw you over?"

"Maybe," I said, "or maybe she was getting a kickback from the insurance company."

"What are you going to do?"

"I'm going to call the insurance company when I get back to The Dusty Attic and see what they have to say." My stomach grumbled, reminding me I needed to eat, and I picked up my menu again. "You two decided what you want yet? I'll order."

Our waitress, Sophie, took our order and informed me, when I asked, that it was Lexi's day off. I'd been hoping to quiz her on her relationship with Mike, but it seemed that wasn't on the agenda for today.

Thankfully, our food didn't take long to arrive, and I waited while Sophie set a bowl of steaming pumpkin soup in front of me. Jenna had ordered lasagna and Monica a chicken and avocado sandwich.

"I've been thinking." I took a spoonful of soup, closing my eyes to savor the creamy richness. "About the case."

"Yeah?" Monica asked, mouth full.

"A couple of things don't add up."

"Oh, I know what you mean!" Jenna piped up. "I've been thinking about it, too."

"Let's hear it then," Monica demanded.

"It's Bruce," I said.

Jenna was nodding, "Yeah. And the borrio bud, right?"

"Right."

"What do you mean?" Monica asked.

"Well, where is it? If Bruce stole it to poison his wife, why haven't the police found it? They questioned him, presumably searched his home. Jackson didn't say anything about finding it. And surely, he'd have to tell you, Jenna, if he did. It's your property, after all."

"I haven't heard any more about it since giving my statement."

"I thought, when I saw his inflamed arm at the Christmas party, that he'd gotten it from the borrio bud plant, but maybe I was wrong. Wendy said he could have gotten it from a reaction to anything."

"It's looking like Bruce isn't the killer," Monica said. "What if whoever stole the plant is the one who took a shot at him?"

"But it doesn't make sense. Why go to all the trouble of framing him for murder and then try to kill him?" I argued. "Bruce has to be involved."

"Or there are two murderers. Maybe Bruce killed his wife. Maybe the attempt on his life was retaliation," Monica said. "Bruce was having an affair. Maybe Whitney was, too. Maybe she left someone behind who loved her and is devastated she's dead?"

"The question is, who? And how did she keep it secret?" I continued eating my soup, my mind going over the possibilities. Whitney could come and go from the Palmer Construction offices as she pleased. It would have been relatively easy for her to meet with someone for a forbidden tryst. I wished now I'd swiped her appointment book when I'd been in her office, but I made a mental note to tell Jackson of our suspicions. He had the resources and would be much better placed than us to trace her footsteps.

CHAPTER
THIRTEEN

My call to the insurance company was very informative, to say the least. I decided my next steps required a face-to-face conversation.

"Gran? Can you mind the store for a bit? I have an errand to run."

"As long as you're back by three," she said, not looking up from her knitting. She'd recently learned the skill, and she held up what appeared to be a moth-eaten riot of colored wool, nodded to herself, and then resumed the click-clacking of the needles. Her tongue poked out of the corner of her mouth in concentration.

"What's happening at three?" I knew I shouldn't ask. She always had something on, something I'd never expect, and for an old lady, she was incredibly active.

"Pole dancing class," she muttered, then frowned when she counted her stitches. "Oh no. There's even more than before."

I ignored the pole dancing comment. "What are you making?"

"It's a surprise."

Shaking my head, I grabbed my purse. "Archie, you stay with Gran. I'll only be half an hour."

Closing the door behind me and buttoning my jacket to my throat to ward off the chill, I headed down the street to Palmer Construction.

"I thought you already found your contract?" Christina said, an annoyed frown on her face.

I gave her a small smile. "I did. I actually wanted to talk to you."

"Oh?" She glanced up from her computer, scanned me up and down before returning her attention back to her screen as if I were nothing but a big fat annoyance. I wonder if she realized she was mimicking Whitney to a tee?

"Yes. I rang Phoenix Feather Insurance today—I need to take out a policy on The Dusty Attic — and they told me you're the representative for Whitefall Cove?"

That got her attention. She visibly brightened, straightened her shoulders, and gave me a warm, welcoming smile. "Well, yes, I am. What sort of cover were you after? Public liability? Building and contents?

Personal? Life?"

"Building and contents for the bookstore," I replied, "and public liability. They also mentioned I could be eligible for magic misuse cover?"

"I'll have to look into that since currently you don't have your witch's license. But I can certainly arrange the building and contents for you today. Let me see if I can pull up the evaluation Whitney did on The Dusty Attic, and take it from there."

"So, Whitney did all the evaluations?" I asked, taking a seat.

"She took care of the onsite inspections and would write up the evaluation and I would fill out the official forms with what she provided. Here it is, found it."

"Interesting." Tapping my fingers on my purse, I mulled over what she'd just told me. Christina was the representative; she was the one pocketing any commissions. How would Whitney benefit by over-inflating the value? "Could I look at the information Whitney provided? Before you typed it up?"

Looking up from her screen, Christina frowned. "Why?"

"Because I think there's an error. My valuation is wrong."

"Oh, we get that a lot," Christina said, dismissing my concern. "Most people think their property is worth more than it actually is."

"I'm the opposite. I think you've overvalued my property."

She sniffed. "Highly doubtful."

"By about one hundred thousand dollars," I stated calmly.

Christina ran a finger around the collar of her blouse, then cleared her throat. "You're right. That sounds like an error. But the problem is..." She paused, and I could see she was struggling to find words. Then she raised a finger and continued on in a rush, "The thing is, Whitney fills out the forms by hand, I type them up, then I throw out the handwritten ones."

"Are you sure?" I pushed. "Because I saw several of those in Whitney's office when I was searching for my contract."

Silence filled the room. I waited, knowing she was lying. Christina swallowed, sweat beading on her forehead, then a slow flush crept up her neck. Quite unexpectedly, she launched herself at me, screaming, "You cow!" Her momentum tipped my chair backward, and we crashed to the floor, Christina on top of me. I wrapped my arms around my head to fend off her blows, but thankfully she didn't know how to throw a decent punch and was slapping at me more than anything else.

I heard a door open and male voices, then Christina was hauled off me. I lay there for a second, catching my breath, before Jackson came into view, crouching by my side.

"You okay?" he asked, taking my arm and helping me up.

"Yeah, I'm fine." Brushing myself off, I turned to look at Christina, who was twisting in Mike's grip, her hair falling out of its bun and hanging around her furious face.

"What did you do?" Jackson asked, standing next to me and watching Christina, too.

"That's just it. I didn't do anything," I replied. "I was questioning an error in the valuation on The Dusty Attic." I told him the rest of the story and he listened attentively before turning his attention to Christina, who had quieted down as I spoke.

"You realize you've just assaulted Harper?" Jackson said in his cop voice. "So, cut the theatrics and let's sort this out like reasonable adults. Harper says she believes there was an error with the valuation of The Dusty Attic. What do you know about that?"

Christina stared at him with stormy eyes, then her face crumpled and she began to cry. I looked from her to Mike, to Jackson and back to Christina again, totally confused by the display of emotion.

"Okay, okay, I did it!" she cried, finally wrenching her arm from Mike's grip. With shaking hands, she smoothed back her hair and straightened her clothes. "I falsified the valuation."

"What?" Mike and I said in unison. I'd totally thought Whitney was behind it.

"Why?" Jackson asked.

"My commission is based on the valuation of the property." She sniffed.

"Yes, but that would mean I'd be paying a higher premium, more than I have to," I pointed out. She shrugged as if she didn't care about that.

"Damn it, Christina." Mike shook his head.

"Is Harper the only one?" Jackson asked. She shook her head no.

"What?" Mike's voice went up three octaves. "Are you kidding me? Christina, how could you do this to me? Shafting my clients?"

Christina cried harder, and I dug in my purse for a tissue, pressing it into her hand.

"I didn't usually alter it so much," she said miserably. "I only added ten grand to the original figure. But then..." She turned to Mike. "It's your fault," she accused him. "You gave Whitney that Christmas bonus and I figured I'd get mine another way, so I adjusted Harper's valuation."

"By a hundred thousand," I muttered, "giving yourself a nice fat commission."

Jackson shook his head. "You're under arrest for fraud. Go take a seat and do not move." He pointed to a chair across the room. He waited until she did as instructed, before reaching into his pocket and pulling out his phone.

"Hey, Liliana." He paused to listen. "Yeah, that sounds great. Listen, can you come on by Palmer Construction? I've just arrested Christina Wallace for fraud. I need you to take her in and book her. I've still got business here."

"Harper, I cannot apologize enough." Mike looked positively ill at this turn of events. "I had no idea this was going on under my nose. Or how long."

"We're going to have to subpoena your records, Mike. Shut down your office," Jackson interrupted.

"Yeah, I figured." He sighed. "That's okay. We close for the week between Christmas and New Year anyway, so I'll just start my holidays a couple of days early."

I placed my hand on Mike's arm. "It's not your fault Mike, although..." I hesitated, wondering if I should say more.

"Although?" he quizzed.

"Well, this ten-thousand-dollar bonus you paid Whitney seems to have created a lot of ill will," I pointed out.

"Not you too." He shook his head and looked at Jackson, who shrugged.

"What?" I asked.

"The ten thousand I gave Whitney was not a bonus

or a gift. It was a loan. To help her establish her own realtor's office. She came to me last month, said her marriage was in trouble and she didn't feel she could go to Bruce with her financial plans. She needed a deposit to lease office space. I gave it to her. I'd always known I stood the chance of losing her, but I thought maybe this was what she needed to get herself back on track. You saw the state of her office, Harper. She was a mess, and that wasn't like her. She needed a fresh start to follow her dreams, and I was happy to help her with that. And I was going to promote Christina to office manager. Damn it. Now I'm down two staff members."

I cleared my throat. "So... not a Christmas bonus then?"

"No."

"Nor blackmail?" I risked a glance at Jackson out of the corner of my eye, wondering if he'd be angry I'd brought it up.

"No. Whitney didn't take that photo. She found it taped to the office door one morning. I don't know who put it there, or why. A warning from my pack, perhaps."

So Jackson had already asked Mike about the photo. Probably why he was here.

"Who is she?" I asked.

"No one you know. A stranger passing through. We hooked up. Then she left town."

"I'm going to need her name and number, Mike," Jackson said, "to corroborate your story."

Mike snorted. "If I had her name or number, I would have called her by now. As I said, we hooked up. Names didn't come into it."

"Is that because she's a fox shifter?" I asked.

"Partly. But honestly, guys, you're reading far more into this than what it was. It was a random hook up. Nothing more."

The office door swung open, and in marched Officer Miles, the icy wind turning her cheeks pink. She smiled at Jackson and then saw me. "Should have known you'd be in the middle of this," she snapped, before crossing to Christina and barking, "Up!"

Christina shot to her feet, face pale, while Officer Miles cuffed her and placed her under arrest before marching her out of the office. "I'll see you back at the station," she said to Jackson, and then she was gone.

———

Thunder rolled overhead, shaking the windows, a flash of lightning briefly illuminating the night sky before plunging us back into darkness. Clutching my umbrella, I battled against the wind as I hurried from my car to Brewed Awakening, the bar where Monica worked. I was meeting Jenna for drinks and quiz night. It was the perfect opportunity to update them on what I'd discovered today. After I returned from Palmer Construction, Gran had scurried off for her pole dancing classes and I'd had a steady stream of customers until late afternoon when the impending storm had chased them away.

I'd just reached the foyer of Brewed Awakening and was shaking the rain from my umbrella when I heard Jackson's voice, only he wasn't speaking to me. Casting a quick glance over my shoulder, I saw him and Officer Miles—Liliana—huddled together on the opposite side of the foyer, peering outside at the downpour. They must have ducked in for shelter, for they showed no signs of intending to move further inside. I was about to call out hello since they hadn't noticed me when I hesitated—Liliana's voice carried, and what she'd just said piqued my interest. Turning my back again, I huddled into my coat and unashamedly eavesdropped.

"So that whole blackmail angle was a wash," she said. I didn't hear what Jackson said. I imagined him nodding in agreement, because she continued, "And so far we've got nothing on the vehicle used in the drive-by shooting. A dark sedan. Does Sims know how many dark sedans are in Whitefall Cove?"

"You've got the three numbers of the license plate, though," Jackson pointed out. "Have you run them?"

"Of course I have." She sounded snippy tonight, and I wondered what had her so riled up. I thought she only used that tone with me and I wanted to chance another look to read their body language, but refrained from doing so. Instead, I pretended to fiddle with my umbrella just in case they busted me.

"Three potential matches," she said. "It's easing. Let's go."

I heard the door open then close, and chanced a peek over my shoulder. Yep, they'd gone. My mind mulled over what I'd just overheard as I hurried inside, waving to Jenna, who sat at the bar, a fancy cocktail in front of her.

"That looks good." I nodded at her drink and she smiled.

"It is delicious." We kissed each other's cheek, and I slid onto the stool next to her. Monica was serving a customer at the other end of the bar, so I waited until she was finished before indicating the cocktail in front of Jenna. She gave me a thumbs up.

"You look like the cat that got the cream." Jenna grinned, sipping her drink.

"I've got so much to tell you!" I shrugged out of my coat and draped it over the back of the bar stool. "But I'll wait until Monica gets here."

I didn't have to wait long. Within seconds Monica was sliding an exotic cocktail in front of me and leaning over the bar to plant a kiss on my cheek. "Merry Christmas." She beamed.

"Merry Christmas!" Jenna and I raised our glasses

in a toast, then I took a sip of my drink. It was nirvana. Sweet, yet not too sweet. I couldn't identify the alcohol, but I could feel the tingling buzz that told me there was a fair amount of it in my drink. I'd have to take it easy. I could easily get drunk with Monica's cocktails.

"Harper was just going to tell us about her day," Jenna said. "Apparently it's been eventful."

Monica laughed. "I don't think you've had a quiet day since you've been back in Whitefall Cove," she joked.

"Well..." I leaned in and the two of them did the same, Monica's dark head, Jenna's blonde one, and my chocolate locks. "Christina Wallace has been falsifying documents to earn herself higher commission from Phoenix Feather Insurance." I nodded my head in a *"what do you have to say about that"* manner. They were suitably shocked. Then I filled them in about the ten thousand dollars not being a Christmas bonus but a business loan for Whitney to open her own realtor office. And Whitney hadn't taken the photo of Mike kissing a strange woman. It had been left anonymously on the door of Palmer Construction.

"You have had a fruitful day," Monica said, wiping down the bar.

"There's more."

"Spill," Jenna demanded.

"On my way in here, I overheard Jackson and

Liliana talking about the shooting. Apparently, they've run that partial number plate and have three potential matches."

"Well, that's good," Monica said, "but you didn't see the car that night, did you?"

"Not really. It approached from behind me, so Bruce was facing it—maybe that's when he noticed the plates? But then the shooting started, and he leaped on me and I was flat on the sidewalk looking at the sky. I couldn't say what type of car it was, what color, nothing really other than it was a car."

"I'll follow up with my informant." Jenna pulled out her phone and shot off a text message. "He should have something for me by now."

"Aren't you going to ask me more about Christina?" I said. "I thought you'd be all over that."

She sighed, shoulders slumping. "Rick has that story. He was coming out of the *Tribune* offices when he saw the police car arrive. He actually got some really good photos of Christina being put into the back. I would have thought he'd have contacted you by now for an interview or a quote." She frowned when I shook my head.

"I'm sorry he beat you to it."

"I'm not worried," she assured me, "because I'm going to break Whitney's story and that is going to get me a Journalist of the Year award."

"Hey, Harper."

I turned to see the young witch I'd sat next to in Drixworths Academy smiling at me. "Hey, Alayna." I smiled in return. "Here for quiz night?"

She nodded. "A bunch of us from class have put a team together." I followed her gaze to a table where at least six witches were gathered. "We were wondering if you'd like to join us?"

"Oh." I was taken aback. "Thank you—" I was about to decline, but Jenna nudged me. "What?" I whispered over my shoulder. I was here with her. I couldn't join another team.

"Jenna can come too," Alayna offered.

"Sure," Jenna agreed before I could stop her. "That'd be fun. Come on, Harper." And before I could protest, Jenna dragged me behind Alayna as she led us to the table of witches. Young witches. Witches who looked like they were twelve years old and had no business being in a bar. Young witches who made me feel decidedly old. "Stop scowling." Jenna elbowed me in the ribs. "And have some fun. It's Christmas. Forget about murder for a while."

"Okay, okay," I grumbled, plastering a smile on my face. We went through introductions and I did my best to remember names, but failed miserably. The others scooched up to let us squeeze two more chairs around their table.

Then I saw Gran, dressed in a slutty Santa outfit, standing behind the podium on the stage and tapping the mic. "This thing on?" she demanded. It was, and she was loud.

"Good evening, Twunkbergers!" A roar of laughter met her words, and I cringed. Why hadn't Gran told me she was MC for the Christmas Quiz? I'd have stayed home.

"Are you ready for some fun?"

The crowd yelled, "*Yes!*"

"Good!" She beamed at them. "Because there's an extra prize on the cards tonight! The winning team will get a lap dance by... drum roll, please... me!" She danced out from behind the podium and twerked at the audience, who hooted and hollered. TWERKED. My eyeballs rolled so far back in my head, I was looking at my spine. I was way too sober for this.

CHAPTER
FOURTEEN

I started my morning with my usual cup of coffee and scorched retinas. Gran was wearing yet another transparent negligee. "If I leak blood from my eyeballs, I am going to come back and haunt you so bad."

She strutted across the kitchen, did a hip thrust, then flung open the refrigerator door, thankfully blocking my view. "You have no appreciation of the female body."

"Nope. I do not," I agreed. Hearing a floorboard creak overhead, I arched a brow. "Who do you have up there?"

"Henry," she said, then straightened and peered at me over the fridge door. "Or is it Adam? Memory isn't what it used to be." She disappeared back into the fridge, then held out her arm, a can of whipped cream clutched in her hand. "Found it!"

Oh God, the visual was alarming. I did not want to think about what Gran intended to do with a can of whipped cream and the man upstairs. She sashayed out of the kitchen, humming to herself, and I rested my head on the table. My hangover gnawed at my insides, making my stomach churn. Last night had been a lot of fun. Gran, as it turned out, was a very talented quiz master, but I'd never been more grateful when our team didn't win. A lap dance from my grandmother was not what I'd consider a prize.

My phone buzzed, and I glanced at the screen. Jenna. "Hey," I picked up the call.

She laughed. "You don't sound so hot."

"How are you not hung over?" I demanded.

"Stronger constitution and you're out of practice," she told me. "This might make you feel better. I've got a lead. On the number plate."

She was right. I immediately forgot my hangover. "You do? What?"

"My informant tells me there's a car that matches that description out at the foxes' compound." The foxes' compound was basically a commune type setup where fox shifters lived, about ten miles out of town.

"Are you thinking what I'm thinking?" I said, draining my coffee.

"That we hit the compound tonight?" she suggested.

"Exactly! We'll take a look under the cover of darkness, see what we can find." And maybe, just maybe, seeing the car might jog something in my memory, something I may not have realized I'd seen. Like the driver.

It was not only dark, but bitterly cold. Jenna picked me up, and we headed out to the foxex' compound. I rubbed my hands together and held them to the vent in her car. "So, this compound," I began, "is it really a compound? With barbed wire and locked gates?"

She shook her head. "I've only been out here once before to cover a story, but no. It's like a rundown trailer park with a bunch of cabins and trailers scattered around a field in no particular order. I'm not sure if fox shifters are pack rats, but this pack is—are they even called a pack? Anyway, they've got junk everywhere. Old car bodies, engines, that type of thing. They seem mechanically minded."

"They're not a pack. The most common term is skulk," I told her. I'd researched them in the bookstore that afternoon.

"Thank you, Encyclopedia Harper." Jenna grinned.

"It's just up here." She pointed through the windscreen.

"Turn off your lights." I pointed to the shoulder of the road. "And pull in here. We'll have to walk in. I don't want them to know we're here."

"Are you forgetting they're foxes? They'll most likely pick up our scent as soon as we set foot on their property." Pulling onto the verge, Jenna turned off the engine and killed the lights.

"Gran gave me these." Digging in the pocket of my parka, I pulled out two small bags wrapped in twine.

"Charms?"

I nodded. "Charms. They won't render us invisible or anything cool, but they will block our scent. Place it against your skin." I handed her one, took my own, and tucked it inside my bra. Flinging open the door, I climbed out, bracing myself against the blast of icy wind. I'd dressed appropriately: black parka, black jeans, black gum boots—it had rained, and I suspected it would be muddy out here—and a black beanie pulled down over my ears.

Jenna was identically dressed. "I feel we need black face paint," she whispered, coming around to my side of the car.

"You think?" I looked at her glowing white face in the moonlight.

"No, I was joking!"

"Oh. Right." I pulled on my gloves, reached back into the car, and grabbed a flashlight.

"Be careful where you point that thing," she warned. "Remember, we don't want them to know we're here. Keep it pointed at the ground and put your hand over it if you see someone coming."

"You've done this before," I said, impressed.

"I'm an investigative reporter," she muttered, leading the way. "Of course I've done this before. Let's go."

It was easy going until we turned down their driveway, and I use that term loosely. The driveway was a muddy track that tried to suck the gumboots off my feet.

"We're leaving footprints," Jenna grumbled, grabbing my arm and pulling me off the track. "We'll be less obvious if we go around the long way."

"How long is the long way?" I asked, already breathless. At least the exercise had warmed me up. I was no longer freezing, despite my breath puffing out in white clouds and my face being numb.

"Just a few feet this way. We'll run parallel to their makeshift road. This way, it's easier to hide if a car comes."

Good point. We walked for another five minutes before Jenna grabbed my arm and pulled me behind a tree. I covered the flashlight with my hand.

"What is it?" I whispered.

"There." She pointed, and I peered around the tree where I could just make out a single light bulb burning over the door of a trailer. I peered closer.

"Is that..." I wondered out loud.

"On bricks?" she supplied. "Yeah." Jenna was right. The foxes' compound resembled a junkyard. Everything I'd expect to find in a house had been dumped here. Old TVs, washing machines, fridges. Not to mention car bodies, even a boat. All rusting, with weeds growing inside some of them.

"They just dump what they don't want literally outside their front door?" I whispered as we inched closer.

"Looks like," she whispered back.

"What a shame." I crouched, eyeballing a sedan parked next to another van. "This place could be really neat if it wasn't for their rubbish."

The door to the trailer opened, and I held my breath. Had they heard me? A man stepped down, looked around, crossed to the car and got something from the glove compartment before going back inside. The light spilling from the trailer briefly illuminated the car, and I squinted at the license plate. Not the vehicle we were looking for.

"Look." Jenna tugged my arm, and I looked to where she was pointing. Across the field was a bonfire, with several people gathered around it.

"Is that Lexi?" I couldn't be sure from this distance.

"Could be." We watched for a few minutes before continuing on. As the minutes ticked past, we found ourselves closer and closer to the bonfire. Music drifted to us on the night breeze and I could see now that the bonfire revelers were dancing.

"It is Lexi," Jenna confirmed, and I stopped again to watch. She looked different outside of the chambray shirt uniform she wore at Bean Me Up. Tonight, she had on a chunky knit sweater in red. The color was very flattering on her. Her hair was down, brushing her shoulders and fanning out behind her as she twirled and swayed to the music. In her hand, a bottle of something—whiskey? Scotch maybe. Some sort of spirit was my guess. She was swigging it straight out of the bottle.

We skirted around the bonfire, weaved in and around the hodgepodge of trailers, cabins, even a tent. I was ready to admit defeat when we saw it. A sedan, parked behind a group of trees away from all the trailers.

"I think this could be it," Jenna whispered, picking up the pace. I tried to keep up, but lost my boot in the mud and face-planted with a whoosh. The flashlight flew out of my hand, arcing through the air before landing with a plop a few feet away.

"Shoot!" Scrambling to my knees, I retrieved my boot and shoved my foot in it, ignoring the squelch of mud oozing through my sock. "Did they see?"

Jenna snatched up the flashlight and turned it off, then stood frozen, watching the horizon. Eventually, she shook her head. "I don't think so."

"Thank goodness." I struggled to my feet and tried to scrape the mud off my front. What a mess.

"Come on." Grabbing my hand, she led the way to the car hidden in the trees. Flicking on the flashlight, she illuminated the license plate. "It's a match." We crept closer, cupped our hands and pressed our faces to the windows to look inside. Nothing. It was empty. Not even a chocolate wrapper on the floor. I was about to try the door when Jenna stopped me. "No! The interior light could come on."

"Darn it." I cursed. "You're right. Okay, well, let's take some photos and report this to the police. Jackson can get a search warrant or whatever it is they need."

We both snapped photos with our phones, then began the long trek back toward the main gate. We drew even with the bonfire, this time on the opposite side. The music still played, but the dancers were gone. I shivered. It was spookier than Halloween out here.

"I've got a real uneasy feeling," I whispered to Jenna.

She clutched my hand in hers. "Me too," she whispered back. "I think they're on to us."

"Do we run?"

"No. Because then *they'd* know that *we* know. Just keep walking. But keep your eyes peeled."

I turned my gaze forward, and that's when I saw them. Glowing eyes in the woods. I blinked, and they were gone. I blinked again, and another set joined the first.

"They've shifted," I said, my voice barely above a whisper.

"I know. Keep going."

We trudged onward, the foxes keeping pace with us in the heavy woods to our right. I was comforted by Gran's charm and knowing they couldn't track us through our scent, but how good was their eyesight? Did they recognize us? Although our thick padded parkas effectively hid our body shapes, our height alone probably screamed the fact that we were female.

"You have Jackson on speed dial, right?" Jenna asked, and I nodded. If they attacked, would I have time to call? It's not as if I could hold out a hand and say *excuse me, do you mind not ripping me to shreds just for a moment while I call for help?*

"Do not panic." Jenna squeezed my hand, and I shot her a look.

"I'm not panicking!"

I was totally panicking. I was about to run screaming toward our car. Or more precisely, where I thought our car was because I couldn't see too well in the dark, and since Jenna had confiscated the flashlight, I had to rely on her to lead the way. City life had made me soft. And knowing a pack—correction—a skulk of foxes was skulking after us was freaking me out big time. I was not the brave witch I wished to be.

"Look." Jenna's calm voice penetrated the haze of terror that was building, and I forced myself to focus on her words. "There's the gate. We get through there and we're off their territory. They'll back down."

"You sure about that?" I asked through clenched teeth, picking up the pace now that I could make out the shadowy silhouette of what I would loosely call a gate. It obviously served no purpose as an actual gate, mere wooden slats that had once borne a resemblance to one.

"I'm hopeful." By the time we cleared the gates, we were power walking and by the time we reached the car, I was at a full-out sprint.

"Get in, get in!" I cried, wrenching open the passenger door and flinging myself inside. Jenna calmly slid behind the wheel, turned the key in the ignition, and executed a perfect U-turn. She waited until we were out of sight of the foxes' compound before flicking on the lights.

I flopped back against the seat, dragging the beanie off my head and clutching it in my hands. "Oh my God. I don't mind admitting that scared the ever-living daylights out of me."

"It got a little intense, didn't it?" Jenna grinned, and I couldn't help but snort out a laugh.

"They were stalking us! Did you see?"

She nodded. "I did. But they didn't hurt us, nor confront us. I think we're okay."

"Next time I have a brilliant idea to go snooping around a fox compound at night, remind me of this, will you? How absolutely intimidating and scary those little foxes can be."

She laughed. "I'll try, but we both know once you've got an idea in your head, there's no stopping you." She had a point. I pulled out my phone and began typing.

"Whatcha doing?" she asked, glancing my way before returning her attention to the road.

"Texting a photo of the car—complete with number plate—to Jackson and telling him where it is."

"Will he get mad we went out there?"

"Probably."

Jenna dropped me home, and I let myself inside, all the while imagining a steaming hot bath waiting for me. I was cold, tired, and filthy, and all I wanted was to soak away my troubles. Archie trotted up the stairs behind me and I told him the entire story while I relaxed with bubbles up to my neck. He sat on the vanity and listened attentively.

CHAPTER
FIFTEEN

Shattered glass was strewn everywhere.

"Someone is ticked off at you," Gran said, standing next to me as we took in the damage to The Dusty Attic.

"Apparently." Sucking in a deep breath, I gathered myself, then called Jackson.

"Oh, you're finally ready to talk to me?" he answered. He'd left me a couple of messages last night, which I'd ignored because I'd turned my phone off and didn't get them until this morning.

"Yeah, yeah," I brushed him off. "Someone has thrown a brick through the window of The Dusty Attic. I know it's not a police emergency or anything. I'm just letting you know."

"Don't touch anything!" he demanded.

"I haven't. I'm outside with Gran."

"How do you know it's a brick, then?"

"Because I can see it through the gaping hole in my storefront." He didn't reply, just a click, and then I was listening to the dial tone.

"I can clean this up and fix the window," Gran offered, but I stopped her.

"Let Jackson see it first. I want it reported. Then you can fix it." I gave her a hug. "Thank you for everything you do for me. I've been so lost without my magic."

She wrapped her arms around me and squeezed tightly. "You've had a bad run, is all. It'll work out, you'll see."

We stood on the sidewalk arm in arm and waited for Jackson, who pulled up with a screech of tires moments later.

"I told you it wasn't an emergency," I said.

"If you kept your nose out of ongoing investigations, maybe this wouldn't have happened," he grumbled, crossing to the door and turning the knob. Of course it didn't open since I hadn't unlocked it yet.

"It's your fault. You said I could help. And now I have a taste for it. I want to get to the bottom of who killed Whitney. Do you think this is related?" I pushed past him and unlocked the door, broken glass crunching under my feet.

He didn't answer, brushing past me as he pulled

on a glove and bent to examine the brick. It was red, the kind you'd find on any building site. Around it was an elastic band and tucked beneath that, a note. No accident then.

"What does it say?" I leaned over his shoulder to read it. The words that jumped out at me had my stomach fluttering. "You're next."

"A threat. So, this wasn't random. Just kids getting up to mischief." I was amazed my voice didn't shake.

"Nope." Shaking open a plastic bag, he placed the brick and note inside before sealing it up. "Evidence. Might get prints off the paper."

"Can I restore order now, Detective?" Gran asked.

"Let me take some photos first." Pulling out his phone, he began documenting the damage.

"Isn't that Officer Miles's job?" I watched as he took shots from every angle imaginable, then the window frame, the broken glass.

"She's busy with something else."

I grasped his arm, forcing him to stop. "Oh, is it the car out at the foxes commune?"

"We'll talk about that later." His tone told me he wasn't happy. At all.

"So, do you know who the car is registered to?" I pressed. Hell, I'd already trespassed, had a brick thrown through my window and a note threatening my life. How much worse could it get?

"It was stolen in Alabama several months ago."

Then he zipped his lips, ignoring the million questions I threw at him until he suddenly grabbed my shoulders and peered into my face. "Do I need to get your Gran to put a silencing spell on you? Just. Be. Quiet."

"You know about silencing spells?" I shot back, then bit my lip. He did look a bit annoyed. I figured I'd pushed him as far as I dared today. Miming zipping my lips, I crossed to the coffeepot. "Coffee?" I asked, then slapped my hand over my mouth. Oops. No speaking.

"Please." He nodded, then crooked his finger at Gran to follow him outside. Seconds later a wave of magic washed over the store, the broken glass remolded itself back into a window. Everything was as it should be. Except I'd just received a death threat. And that got me thinking. What if the bullet that hit Bruce that night hadn't been meant for him at all? What if they were aiming for me and were a lousy shot? But why? Why would someone want me dead?

Gran and Jackson were talking out front, and I pushed open the door to join them. Jackson was patting Gran's arm, and I frowned. "What's going on?"

"Detective Ward," Gran used his title, which told me she was annoyed at him and Gran didn't often get annoyed at people, "wants you to close your store."

"What?" I shifted my attention to Jackson, who

was rubbing his hand around the back of his neck, his face a picture of concern.

"Harper," he began. "Let's go to Bean Me Up and talk about this. Mrs. Brewer, would it be a huge imposition if you looked after things here until Harper returns?"

I bit my lip to stifle the giggle that threatened to spill out. He was giving it back to Gran as good as he got. I wondered if he knew she hated being called Mrs. Brewer? I suspected he did, which was why he'd just done it.

"Fine," she huffed, "I'll open up. You two kids talk. And for God's sake, call me Alice."

"Only if you call me Jackson." His grin was warm and endearing and a part of me melted inside. *What are you doing, Harper Jones? He's taken!* He may have been six foot four of deliciousness with his dark hair and green eyes, but he was not mine to drool over.

"I'll bring you back a double shot macadamia almond milk latte," I promised, and her face brightened. Jackson guided me across the road with his hand on the small of my back and, despite my better intentions, I enjoyed every second.

"Hot chocolate?" he asked after pulling out a chair and making sure I was seated comfortably. This time we weren't near the window, but tucked far away from view.

I shook my head. "I think today calls for a cappuccino."

"Coming right up." He joined the queue at the counter and I absently stared at his denim-clad rear end before catching myself and turning my attention to Lexi, who was back behind the counter this morning. She may have been small, but she was fast, hustling like a champion. Jackson placed our order, then returned, sitting opposite me.

"I'm serious about what I told your gran," he said, those green eyes so intent on me I wanted to squirm in my seat.

"But... it's almost Christmas. I can't close my store now."

"You've received a direct threat to your life."

"Thank you, Captain Obvious," I grumbled, and he laughed. I didn't think I'd seen him laugh before, and my own lips curled into a smile at his apparent humor.

"Let me talk to Gran," I said. "If I had my own powers, I could cast a protection spell, but," I shrugged my shoulders, "I'm as effective as a human right now. Maybe Gran could make me a protection charm."

"Do those things work?"

"To be honest, I'm wondering that myself. Gran made us charms last night so the foxes couldn't pick up our scent."

"You think a fox did this? Followed you back?" A

lecture on trespassing out at the foxes compound was not forthcoming, for which I was grateful.

"It's a possibility. But we were careful. We had the charms, and Jenna had taken off her plates just in case they saw her car." An awful thought hit me, and I pulled out my phone. Jenna answered on the third ring. "Oh, thank God." I breathed in relief. It had occurred to me that if the foxes had identified the car, they would have gone after Jenna, not me.

"Harper? What's going on?" she asked.

"I was just checking on you," I replied, my eyes on Jackson's face as he watched me. "Someone threw a brick through The Dusty Attic's window last night with a threatening note and I had a moment of panic that someone followed us back from—" I stopped, spotting Lexi approaching with our drinks.

"Are you okay?" Jenna asked,

"Yep, I'm all good. I've gotta go," I told her, "but I'll check in with you in a bit, okay?" Not giving her the chance to reply, I hung up.

"Here we go, two cappuccinos." Lexi slid two mugs onto the table, a Christmas tree outlined in the froth.

"Thank you," Jackson and I said in unison. I waited until she'd walked away before leaning toward Jackson. "Did you see that?"

"What?"

"Red dust on the back of her jeans," I murmured, "like she wiped her hands on her pants."

He swiveled just in time to see Lexi round the counter, blocking her bottom half from view.

"You're sure?"

"It looked like red dust to me," I said, "but it could be anything. Cocoa powder, perhaps? Although seriously, it looked red." I pinned him with a look. "Can't you take a sniff of the brick and, you know, follow the trail?"

"Sniff the brick? Why would I do that?" His eyebrows shot into his hairline at my suggestion, and I frowned.

"Because you're a wolf shifter?" *Duh.*

He shook his head. "I'm not a wolf shifter."

"You're not?" Well, that was a surprise. I tried to think who had told me that little snippet. Without my powers, I couldn't tell one supernatural from another, so I was totally at a loss. "What *are* you then?"

"I'm a necromancer."

I almost shot coffee out of my nose. A detective who could speak to the dead? Perfect! "No wonder you're a detective." I coughed, snatching up a napkin to pat at my face where I'd snorted my drink. "You must have an incredibly high success rate."

"You missed a spot." Taking the napkin from me, he dabbed at my cheek before leaning back in his chair. "Not really. I can only talk to the dead if they want to talk to me."

"Why wouldn't they?"

"A dozen reasons. Some don't know they're dead. Some are traumatized by their death and are caught in a pattern re-living it. Hard to get through to those. Some just don't like me and refuse to speak. And others have already moved on, and their spirit is no longer reachable."

"You've tried to talk to Whitney, I assume?" I leaned forward and captured his hand, realized what I'd done and immediately released it with a muttered, "Sorry."

"I have tried, yes. So far, nothing. I suspect she's already crossed over."

"Darn. On two counts." I took another sip of my coffee. "This tastes different today." I looked down into the contents of frothy goodness, wondering if they were using a different blend. I did not expect Jackson to knock the cup out of my hand, sending it flying to the floor, where it shattered. "Hey!" I protested. "Why did you do that?"

"Really?" He looked at me as if I had two heads and the penny dropped. He thought I'd been poisoned. *Wait, what?*

I felt the blood drain from my face. My hand went to my throat.

"It's okay. Don't panic." Jackson hadn't touched his drink yet. It was okay for him to say, don't panic. He hadn't just consumed poison.

The people in the queue had turned and were

staring at us. A waitress approached, dishcloth in hand.

"No. Stay back," Jackson barked, and the poor confused girl looked at him like he'd lost his mind. Snatching up a handful of napkins from the dispenser on our table, he dropped them onto the coffee puddle, then shook open another evidence bag. How many of those did he have stuffed in his jacket pocket?

"I'll get this tested," he said to me, his voice low. He slid the evidence bag, sealed with soggy napkins, into his pocket, then turned to the waitress with a smile. "Sorry. My fault, talking with my hands again. Here, I'll clean it up." He held out his hand for the dishcloth, but the girl clutched it to her chest.

"I can't let you do that, sir," she said. "I'll get fired."

"Fair enough," he soothed. "Tell you what, you go get a trash can or something to put the broken pieces in and I'll start cleaning up. We can do it together."

She nodded and hurried off and I whispered, "Is that wise? Won't you get poisoned too?"

"Only if ingested," he reminded me. I sat and watched while he and the waitress cleaned the mess. I had an hour. If he was right and my coffee was laced with borrio bud, I had one hour to live, and then my heart would simply stop.

"Will it hurt?" I whispered, my fear real. I did not want to die. I had a bookstore to run.

Although I'd whispered the words, Jackson heard

me and straightened, then dropped to one knee beside my chair and clasped one of my hands in both of his. "No," he whispered back, "but I will not let it happen. There has to be an antidote."

I hoped he was right, because dying would suck.

CHAPTER
SIXTEEN

"You did great!" Jackson beamed at me as we crossed the road back to The Dusty Attic.

"What do you mean?" I was in a daze at my impending death—so much to do and so little time. Was there a cure for borrio bud poisoning? I hadn't researched that far, and the book in which I'd found it mentioned was at home, which meant I'd lose precious minutes trying to retrieve it.

"I think she bought it." He seemed thrilled, and I stopped and frowned at him. "Who bought what?"

He looked at me, shook his head, muttered, "Oh boy," then grabbed my upper arm and pulled me inside the bookstore. Closing the door firmly behind us, he glanced around. Half a dozen customers browsed the shelves. His eyes landed on the red velvet curtain and he dragged me over to it, pulling it aside to usher me into the storeroom.

"What's going on?" I asked, thoroughly confused. "Shouldn't we be looking for an antidote? Not standing around in my storeroom."

"You're not dying," he told me, crossing his arms over his chest. "Sorry, there wasn't time to give you a heads up. The idea came to me on the spur of the moment."

I slapped his arm. Hard. He didn't react, but my palm stung and I muttered, "Ow," as I rubbed it against my pants leg. "Explain," I demanded.

"You saw red brick dust on Lexi's jeans," he began.

"So?" I cut in and he gave me that look, that one that said *I will not continue if you keep interrupting*. Rolling my eyes, I clamped my lips together and waited.

"Lexi is a fox shifter. She lives out at the fox commune," he continued.

"She does. I saw her there last night," I agreed.

"Right. And the car that was used in the shooting was found there too. So, she's involved—either directly or indirectly."

"Right." I nodded. "But what was that whole pretending I'd been poisoned thing?"

"A hunch."

"Elaborate!" I waved a hand in the air, frustrated that he was taking so long to get to the point.

"We haven't found the plant yet. Only the person who used it to kill Whitney knows where it is. My reaction—knocking your cup to the floor and taking samples of the coffee? The killer would know why we did that—because we suspected your drink had been poisoned. To anyone else, it would look like I'd merely knocked your cup over."

"I'm not following," I admitted.

"If Lexi is involved, she'd know she *didn't* poison your coffee, right?"

"Right."

"So, what would you do if you were the killer who poisoned Whitney, but now it looked like someone else had been poisoned with the plant you stole?"

"I'd go check on that plant and see if someone had stolen it from me," I shot back. Then the penny dropped. "Oh!"

"Oh indeed."

"So why are we standing in here when we should be following Lexi?"

"Good point. Let's go."

I followed him out of the storeroom and back into my store. "We have the perfect vantage point here," he said, standing back from the window, close enough to see out but far enough back we couldn't be seen from outside. Gran approached, and I hugged her, so very glad I wasn't dying after all.

"What's up with you?" she asked, and Jackson shot me a warning glance.

"Nothing," I replied. "Spilled my drink and didn't get my caffeine hit." It was almost true. Gran shuffled off and was back a minute later with a steaming mug of coffee for both of us. "I'm going to let you off, just this once, for not bringing me my double shot macadamia almond milk latte as promised. I figure something happened. You both look like you could use this more than me."

"Thank you."

"Don't mention it," she said in return, then spied the same young man who'd been in the other day, the one with his hair in a bun, and she hustled over to him, her hips swaying.

"Back so soon, gorgeous?" she cooed. Rather than running away in fear, he turned to her with a big, warm smile on his face.

"She's a character," Jackson said, taking a sip of his drink.

"She is," I agreed. Then movement outside caught my eye. "Look. It's Lexi!" We watched as Lexi stepped out of Bean Me Up. Standing on the sidewalk, she looked left, then right, seemingly unsure which way to go. I took a big mouthful of coffee, then set the mug on the windowsill. Jackson's car was outside. As soon as Lexi headed off, we'd follow her. Well, I assumed that was the plan; otherwise, this entire ruse was for nothing.

"Oh my God," I breathed, "is that Mike Palmer?"

It was a rhetorical question, but Jackson answered anyway, "Yep." We watched as Mike approached, slid a hand around Lexi's neck, and lowered his head to kiss her. She wound her arms around his neck and returned the kiss. For quite some time.

"So, it *was* Lexi in that photo," I said, "which means Mike lied to us. To you—the police!"

Jackson glanced at me. "One thing you'll learn with investigative work, Harper, is that everyone lies. It's a given."

"Oh." I felt a little foolish. Lying wasn't something I did, well, outside the little white lie here and there to save someone's feelings. Like the cupcakes Aunt Mildred used to make. I'd lied and said they were delicious when, in fact, they weren't.

Finally, Mike and Lexi came up for air and I cocked my head. "Why now? Why this public display of affection when obviously they've been keeping their relationship a secret?"

"I think it's for our benefit."

"What? They know we're watching?"

"Possibly. But even if we weren't, there are plenty of people on the street who are now gossiping about the sizzling kiss they just planted on each other. And, as you pointed out, it proves that Mike lied in an active police investigation."

I gasped. "She's throwing him under the bus!" Grabbing Jackson's arm, I practically jumped up and down on the spot. "I'm right, aren't I? She was worried you were on to her, so now she's outed their relationship, and thrown suspicion onto Mike because she knew you'd talked to him and he'd lied about it being her in that picture."

"And if you were keeping a relationship secret in this town and were under scrutiny, what would you do?"

"Lie low. Not see each other for a while," I answered.

"Not meet each other in broad daylight, in the middle of the street, and kiss."

"It's a diversion. She's hoping to throw you off. Is it working?"

It was his turn to sigh as he stroked his fingers over his stubbled jaw. "To be honest, I'm not sure what's going on, but it all looks very suspicious. The car from the shooting is being towed to the station for forensics to go over. I'm confident we'll find traces of gunpowder. Maybe even the shell casing, if they were careless enough."

"But the car was stolen, and we don't know who drove it the night they shot Bruce."

"We'll see if we can't find a fingerprint. If they're

smart, they'll have wiped the whole car down, but there's usually something left behind, some small missed clue. It's our job to find it."

Lexi cupped Mike's face in her hands, reached up on tiptoes to softly kiss his lips, gave him a big smile, then went back inside Bean Me Up. My disappointment was palpable. "Maybe it isn't her. Who poisoned Whitney," I clarified. "She's not running to check on the plant."

"Give it time. We surprised her today. Keep an eye on her, will you? You've got the perfect vantage point. Call me if she leaves."

"You're going?" I'd been hyped up to follow Lexi and nail her for murder. Now I just felt deflated. A day spent in my store seemed boring in comparison.

He nodded to his phone where a text had just arrived. "The car's in forensics. I want to go check it out. I'm going to send Liliana down to talk to Lexi, see if we can't get a sample of that red dust from her jeans and tie her to the vandalism of The Dusty Attic at least. And I need to bring Mike in for a chat. She'll be expecting that."

"You're playing her?" I liked the idea of that, for I hadn't suspected Lexi capable of throwing a brick through my window and threatening me. I'd thought she was a nice young woman, friendly and warm. To learn otherwise was a shock.

"Two can play at her game and I've been playing a

whole lot longer." He winked, waved goodbye to Gran, and left. I watched as he climbed into his car and drove away.

"You like him." Gran slid an arm around my waist and joined me by the window.

"I don't," I protested automatically. But the truth was, I did like him. And couldn't have him because he belonged to someone else and I would not do to Liliana what Simon had done to me. Ever. My relationship with Jackson Ward was and always would be platonic.

"It won't last with her," Gran assured me, and I wasn't sure if she was in my head reading my mind or if she was guessing.

"Gran, you can't say things like that. They're together. In love."

"Together? Yes. In love? Doubtful. At least he isn't. His aura is all wrong for a man in love." And despite it being wrong, a little seed of hope planted itself, and I hated myself for it.

"Did you know he's a necromancer?" I asked, steering the conversation away from Jackson Ward's heart and who he did or did not love.

"Is he?" Gran seemed surprised by this news and I looked at her suspiciously. She had to know, didn't she? Her magic would have alerted her to the fact, so why lie about it? A little white lie to protect me? But why? So many lies and so many questions.

Archie appeared, rubbing around my ankles and meowing. "Hey, boy!" I picked him up and snuggled my face into his fur. "You wouldn't lie to me, would you? No," I crooned, dropping kisses on top of his head, "of course you wouldn't."

"Store's all yours," Gran announced, collecting her purse. "I'm going to art class."

"Art class? I didn't know you were taking art classes."

"Today is real life sketching day." She nodded, eyes gleaming.

"Real life? As in?"

"Nude." She shrugged into her coat. I shook my head at the thought of my gran sketching someone in the nude—that poor model. She nipped that notion in the bud at the door when she casually threw over her shoulder, "Can't be late. I'm the model."

———

The bell above the door jingled, and I glanced up from where I was ringing up a customer to see Jenna bustle inside, her face flushed from the cold.

"Hey." I smiled in greeting. "I won't be a sec." Turning my attention back to the middle-aged woman who'd just purchased a cookbook, I swiped her card, carefully wrapped her book in tissue paper, and placed it in a paper bag before handing it to her. "Merry

Christmas and thank you for shopping at The Dusty Attic."

"Business looks like it's going well," Jenna commented when I came around from my desk to hug her.

"It is. But then it's only been a few days," I pointed out. "Plus, you know, Christmas. What brings you by?"

"I was down at the police compound lot, trying to get a quote. Saw them tow in the car from the foxes compound so knew they must've been reasonably confident it was involved in the shooting."

"Jackson said something about testing it for gunpowder residue?"

"Yeah, that's what I thought. For Bruce to have seen it and get a partial number plate, it had to have been heading west on Main Street, which means the shooter had to be the driver, or a passenger sitting directly behind the driver."

"How do you know all this stuff?" I said, impressed with my friend's skills.

"Duh, it's my job." She grinned. "Anyway, I think they found something."

"Really?" That caught my attention, and I glanced around, wishing my customers would clear out so we could examine the crime board.

"Lots of forensic bags," she said, "but I was too far away to see what they were collecting. I did see one forensic guy pluck something from the headrest, so I'm guessing a hair."

"That could give us the driver!" I clasped both of her hands in excitement. We were getting close. I could feel it. I filled her in on this morning, on the red dust on Lexi's jeans that could potentially tie her to the vandalism of my store and threat to me. Plus, the outing of her relationship with Mike. I'd seen Officer Miles arrive at Bean Me Up not long after Jackson left. She wasn't inside for long, but after she left, Lexi stepped out, stopping to glare at The Dusty Attic before going back into the coffee shop.

"I thought the club could meet tonight?" Jenna suggested. "Maybe Jackson could come along?"

"Oh, has your book club started?" A customer who'd been perusing the shelves behind Jenna turned around, face alight.

"Sorry!" I shook my head. "No. No, the book club won't be starting until the new year," I explained.

"Well, what club is she talking about?" The woman rudely pointed to Jenna, and I closed my eyes. Lord, please save me from nosy customers. "A swingers' club." It was the first thing that came into my head and even as the words fell out, I cringed.

"Really?" The woman looked surprised and a little bit curious.

Jenna saved me. "No. She's joking, Mrs. Leeds. It's a meeting to plan the book club. We were thinking we'd narrow the focus, make it a mystery book club, and we need to choose what book to start with and order in enough copies and arrange logistics. That type of thing. Don't worry, when the book club is ready to launch, you'll hear about it."

"Oh, okay then. A mystery book club sounds marvelous." And off she went, eager to share the little snippet of information she'd just garnered with her friends.

"Thank you," I whispered, miming wiping my hand across my brow and shaking off the sweat.

"You're welcome. But I was serious. We should meet."

"I agree. Eight o'clock, here. I'll let Monica and Jackson know."

CHAPTER
SEVENTEEN

I couldn't believe it. They'd all stood me up. Okay, stood me up was probably unfair. Jackson had said he was working but would try to call in. Monica had picked up an early shift at Brewed Awakening and couldn't make it at all. Jenna called to say she'd caught a break on the impounded car. Turned out it had been used in a robbery in East Dondure and she was writing up her story to hit tomorrow's paper. And Gran? Gran had a date with the man-bun guy from the bookstore, and there was no way she was giving that up.

So here I was, home alone. Tossing my coat on the sofa, I plopped onto the cushions with a sigh. It was rare for me to be home without Gran, and the house felt weird without her. I heard the squeak of the cat door, little feet padding down the hallway, then Archie appeared, another mouse in his mouth.

"Archie!" I screeched, jumping up onto the sofa and waving my arms like a demented banshee. "Take it out, take it out!"

Archie sat, looked at me, and set the mouse down on the floor between his front paws. Oh God. He let it go. Which meant it could easily hide anywhere in the house. There was no winning in this situation. Tiptoeing the length of the sofa, I leaped to an armchair, then threw my leg over the side and bolted out the door, skidding down the hallway.

In the kitchen, I threw open cupboard doors, searching for something to catch the mouse with. That was my plan. Catch the mouse. Release it outside. Not directly outside. Archie would probably catch it and bring it straight back in. I'd take it for a drive, past the town limits, let it go out there. And then I felt bad because what if he had a little mouse family and I was taking him away from them, never to be seen again? Holy guacamole, there was no winning in this scenario.

Finally finding a plastic container and a matching lid, I examined it, noticing the airtight fit. Damn it. The mouse would suffocate. With jerky movements, I put the container on the bench, grabbed a knife and stabbed holes in the lid, muttering under my breath the whole time.

"Archie," I grumbled, heading back to the living room, "didn't I tell you no more critters? I swear I said no more critters. I thought we had an understanding. Don't you understand that I do not cope with critters? At all."

The sight that greeted me had me screaming out loud and dropping the container where it bounced across the floor and rolled under the coffee table. Clapping a hand over my mouth, I eyeballed the naked man in my living room, then quickly spun, presenting him with my back. "Who are you?" I demanded, "and where are your clothes?"

"Sorry about that," he replied, his voice as smooth as silk. "I'm a friend of Esmerelda Higginbottom's, and I've been tasked with keeping an eye on you." I heard a rustling, then he said, "You can turn around now."

I did. He held a cushion in front of his groin. I closed my eyes and tried to gather my thoughts.

"You're saying Drixworths Academy is spying on me?" I wanted, no, *needed*, clarification, because if this was true... well, it was outrageous. Did they spy on all their students? What sort of place were they running? And was my magic license in worse jeopardy than I initially thought?

"Not Drixworths, *per se*." His lips curled, and I was quite taken with the way they lifted at the corners, and the way his eyes twinkled.

"So, you're saying Esmerelda Higginbottom—Izzy—asked you to spy? On me?"

"Not spy. Keep an eye on," he confirmed.

I snorted. "I don't see the distinction between keeping an eye on someone and spying. In my book, they're the same."

"Izzy sensed trouble. A darkness was following you and she was worried for you—especially since you don't have your magic to defend yourself. And it appears she was right to be concerned. Implicated in a murder? A brick thrown through your window?"

"Pfft, I've got it all under control, so you can just run along and tell Izzy that everything here is fine. I don't need you spying on me. Especially as a mouse." I shuddered. "You've no idea how much I dislike mice."

"Oh, I've got a fair idea," he drawled, "and believe me, I have no desire to be captured by your familiar again either. I'm going to have bruises." He ran a hand around his ribcage, where red welts were forming from Archie's teeth.

"Serves you right," I grumbled, feeling no sympathy. "Can you please leave? And tell Izzy I don't need a protective detail. Although I can't see how a mouse shifter is going to be much protection. Maybe next time send a tiger?"

I held open the front door, averting my eyes when he tossed the cushion back on the sofa and strode outside, naked as a jaybird, then transformed back into a mouse, scampering down the garden path. Closing the door, I flicked the lock, then eyeballed the cushion. "That's going to need washing," I muttered, picking it up by the corner and carrying it to the washing machine. I continued my rant to Archie. "Did you know he was a shifter? Is that why you caught him and brought him in? In which case—thank you, but on the other hand, a mouse! Yuk."

I stopped and eyeballed Archie who'd followed me and now sat watching me with his big solemn golden eyes. "I wish you could talk to me." I squatted and stroked his fur. "That would make this so much easier, hmm?" He rubbed his face against my hand and purred. "It was probably a good thing that Gran wasn't home," I continued with my one-sided conversation, "because there's no way she'd have let a naked man out of this house. Oh, no. She'd have dragged him upstairs and locked him in her bedroom and then there'd have been all sorts of trouble. Although clearly, I'm going to have to speak to Izzy about this invasion of privacy."

Climbing the stairs, I ran a bath and poured myself a glass of wine. In the end, I held my own murder club meeting. Lying in the bath, glass of wine in hand, candles flickering, I stared at the ceiling and tried to piece everything together, only it was jumbling in my head and I needed my crime board to make sense of it all. Pulling on my jeans, boots, and a Christmas themed jumper that Gran had left on the bed for me, I hurried back downstairs, grabbed my keys and bag and headed out. Archie stayed right on my heels.

Parking out front of The Dusty Attic, I glanced at my watch. It was getting late, and while the street was aglow with Christmas lights, no one was around. I'd expected carolers, a fake Santa having his photo taken with all the kids, late night shopping, eggnog, and smiles, yet... nothing. Where were the Christmases I remembered as a child? Had Whitefall Cove lost its Christmas spirit? Yet another mystery to ponder.

Making sure to lock the door behind me, I flicked on the lights and rubbed my hands together. It was freezing in here—again. "Damn this thermostat," I muttered, hurrying to the storeroom where, sure enough, the switch was off. Flicking it back on, I pulled out my phone and called Burt Reynolds. No time like the present to sort this out, not that it was his fault. I'd been meaning to call him back ever since he came in and looked at it.

"Burt? Hi, this is Harper Jones from The Dusty Attic. Sorry, I've been meaning to call about the thermostat here. Can you please go ahead and order a new one? It's still turning off on its own. Thanks. Bye." Voicemail left, I hustled back to the main part of the store and moved the bookshelf hiding the crime board.

"Okay," I said to Archie, "where were we?" Archie meowed and scratched at the arm of one of the armchairs. "Oh, you want me to turn that, so you can sit and watch? Okay then." Chuckling to myself at the image of doing my cat's bidding, I spun the chair around and Archie immediately jumped up and sat regally, like a king on his throne, examining the crime board.

I tapped the picture of Bruce. "He's our number one suspect for killing Whitney," I told him. "He had the most to gain from her death. He had motive. But opportunity? That's a little dodgy. Jackson told us the only coffee in Whitney's stomach contents was the one she'd consumed from Bean Me Up. Bruce didn't go near that coffee when he dropped into her office, so how could he have gotten the poison into it?"

Archie meowed, and I nodded. "I agree. He didn't do it." Picking up a red marker, I crossed out Bruce's photo.

"Then we have Mike Palmer." I tapped Mike's photo and Archie's eyes zeroed in on it. "No motive that I can work out. We thought Whitney was blackmailing him, but it turns out that was false. The ten thousand dollars was a loan to lease a shop for her realtor business. Jackson confirmed Whitney had rented a one-room office space at Whitefall Towers. And again, no opportunity. Christina carried the coffees in. Mike took his and returned to his office. No time to take the lid off Whitney's cup, administer the poison, put the lid back on, all in full view."

I took Archie's meow as agreement, crossed out Mike's photo and moved on.

"Wendy Haley. Whitney's best friend. Motive aplenty since Wendy was having an affair with Whitney's husband and was also pregnant with his child. She's a witch, so there's a possibility she knew about the borrio bud plant, and she's a nurse, so she'd understand the effects the plant would have. Opportunity?" I tapped the marker against my lips, thinking. "She brought in muffins. She may have slipped the poison into Whitney's coffee then, assuming the coffee was unattended. I was with Whitney when the coffee arrived. She didn't take it with her into her office. I was there, oh, ten minutes, tops. But Christina was at the reception desk where the coffee was still sitting when I left. Hmmm. Doubtful that Wendy could have administered the poison but not out of the realm of possibility, especially if Christina left her desk for a bathroom break or something."

I marked Wendy's photo with a question mark. I felt it was more of a long shot, but I needed to know more of Christina's movements before I could rule her out. I glanced at Archie, tapping the marker on Christina's photo. "This brings us to Christina. Motive? Jealousy. Absolutely. She was in a rage about the Christmas bonus. Why Whitney lied about it, I do not know, but Christina truly believed Whitney had received a massive Christmas bonus and she was furious about it. Mad enough to kill?" I paused, and Archie meowed. "I agree. We can't rule her out."

Here I was, conversing with my cat like it was the most natural thing in the world. "Okay, well, let's look at opportunity. Yes, absolutely she could have added the poison to the coffee. All the cups were clearly labeled, so she could have slipped the poison in on the way back from Bean Me Up. But..." I paused, pointing the marker at Archie, who cocked his head. "How did she know about the borrio bud plant? She's a brownie. Are they into gardening? Horticulture?"

Archie meowed and stretched, pointing a paw toward the bookshelves. Of course! Look it up. Running up the spiral staircase to the mezzanine level, I ran my eyes along the books until I spied what I wanted. An old leather-bound edition of the encyclopedia of species. Hurrying back to Archie, I perched on the edge of the chair and flicked through the pages until I found the information on brownies. Thankfully, they'd evolved from the dirty-looking creatures depicted in the book, but my general understanding of their species was correct. They were a domestic spirit who excelled at—enjoyed even—household chores.

"You would think that Christina would have been beside herself at the state of Whitney's office, wouldn't you? I mean, it was a mess, and as a brownie,

I'd imagine Christina would have been compelled to clean it up."

"Meow," Archie chimed in.

He patted the page with his paw and I read what he was pawing at. "If angered, they can sometimes turn malicious." I patted Archie on the head. "Malicious enough to kill, do you think? And she was falsifying official paperwork to scam the insurance company into paying her higher commissions. That could be another motive. Maybe Whitney found out? Although, Whitney's head wasn't in the game recently. She was distracted. Lost my keys. I doubt she was paying much attention to what Christina was up to."

Closing the book, I put it on my desk and returned to the crime board, putting a question mark on Christina's photo. "Let's finish going through our suspects and then see if we can narrow it down after." Archie settled himself into a loaf position, front paws tucked under, eyes on the board, waiting for me to continue.

"So finally, we have Lexi. The barista who made the coffees that morning. Motive? None that I know of. We know Whitney could be a bit of a cow and there's the possibility that she'd been rude to Lexi at some point, but Lexi said she'd rarely had any interaction with Whitney. It was Christina who bought Whitney's coffees. And even if Whitney had gotten Lexi off side, poisoning her is a tad extreme, don't you think?" Archie didn't respond, so I continued, "So, no real motive. Opportunity? I guess it could be done. The coffee machine would have hidden Lexi from view while she was making the drinks, so yes, she could have added the poison then." I added a question mark to Lexi's photo.

Standing off to the side of the crime board, I studied it and Archie meowed. Twice.

"Yes, I agree, we're not taking into consideration the shooting. Was it related? Or are they two separate crimes? Either way," I pointed to Wendy's photo, "Wendy couldn't have been the shooter because she was at work that night. She was on duty when Bruce was brought in. Plus, the car was found at the foxes' compound. Yes, maybe she had an accomplice or hired someone, but that would be easy for the police to verify and, despite her having an affair with her best friend's husband, I sense that Wendy's feelings for him are real. I don't think she wants him dead." I drew a cross over the question mark on her photo.

"Let's revisit Christina." I paused, thinking. "Bruce works at the bank. Did he know about her scam? But if he did, he would have told the police, surely? That brings us to Lexi again."

I pulled her photo off the board and sat on the edge of Archie's chair, studying the image. "She had opportunity, but no motive. But the car that was involved in Bruce's shooting was found at the foxes' compound—where Lexi lives. That's the only thing we've got that ties her to this. And let's not forget the red dust I saw on her pants today. That's a potential match to the brick thrown through my window. She's involved somehow."

Archie jumped down and padded over to the crime board before stretching up on his back legs and patting at Mike's photo. "Of course!" I cried. "The secret relationship with Mike. He lied about it. Someone else knew about it. Someone took that photo of the two of them together and left it on his office door. As a threat? Yet today—after Jackson pretended I'd been poisoned—she met Mike outside, in full view of everyone, and kissed him. Or he kissed her. Whatever, they kissed. They knew they'd be seen. So why now? Why go public today?"

Archie came back and rubbed around my legs, then head-butted my shin. "You're right. Only one way to find out."

I had to visit Mike Palmer.

CHAPTER
EIGHTEEN

Mike lived in an ordinary-looking house on an ordinary-looking street. I don't know why I was surprised or what I'd been expecting. Perhaps seeing that fox shifters lived in a commune-type setup, I'd expected wolf shifters to be the same. They weren't. Luckily, his address had been listed in the local directory and had been easy to find. Parking out the front, I was walking down his front path when I heard it. Shouting. I picked up my pace, hurrying to the front door, then leaning around to peek through the window.

Mike and Lexi were inside, yelling at each other. I held my breath and eavesdropped, watching through the window.

"I should have known!" Mike threw his hands in

the air, marched away and then rounded back. "Foxes can't be trusted!"

Lexi laughed, a nasty, evil sound. "Oh, but you were willing to overlook that, weren't you, old man? You didn't care at all as long as you were getting a piece of this!" She ran her hands up and down her body, taunting him. I winced at the old man dig. So did Mike. He crumpled, his face lost all its anger, and he stared at her with such utter sadness I felt tears well in my eyes.

"Why Lexi?" he pleaded, "Why? I love you. I thought you loved me, too."

"Love? Pfft! Don't get me wrong. The sex was great —older men know what they're doing, and you did it oh, so well. But that's all it was. I don't love you. I don't even care about you." Mike physically winced at the verbal barb. How awful. I swung away from the window and leaned against the wall with my hand over my heart. I could feel Mike's pain through the bricks, palpable, pulsing, a twisted mess of emotion. He'd given Lexi his heart, and she was shredding it.

It was quiet for a moment, then he said, voice devoid of emotion, "You said you were going? Then go. I don't want you here. I don't want you in my house. I don't want to see you again. Ever."

"You won't," she assured him. "I'm leaving town."

"Go then."

"I'm going." The front door flung open, and Lexi

marched out. She stopped when she saw me, drilled me with a hard look, then strode down the path without a word. I hadn't seen another car out front so wondered how she got there, but the front door closing drew my attention back to Mike.

"Wait." I knocked softly, and the door opened, Mike gripping the frame as if he didn't have the strength to hold himself up.

"Now's not a good time, Harper," he said.

Ignoring him, I pushed my way inside, waited for Archie to follow before closing the door and pointing to the sofa. "Sit." Both Archie and Mike obeyed.

"I guess you overheard that?" He flopped his head back and stared up at the ceiling.

"I did. And I'm sorry," I said, taking a seat on the opposite end of the sofa, Archie in the middle.

Mike turned his head to look at me. "Should have known it was too good to be true." Tears glistened in his eyes and my heart broke for him.

"You loved her?"

He nodded. "I did. Stupid mistake. I told myself not to. I warned myself she was trouble. But I couldn't help it... I did it, anyway."

"We don't get to choose who we fall in love with." I nodded agreement.

"That's right." He pinned me with his gaze. "Your man cheated on you, right? That must have hurt."

"It did." But not as much as the pain I could feel

rolling off Mike in waves.

"But you're here, starting over, surviving." And I knew what he needed—he needed hope. At this moment, he needed reassurance that he wouldn't die from this pain, that he would love again, that it was entirely possible that one day, he'd be happy.

"We were at the university's Christmas Ball," I began. "It was a big deal. Fancy dresses, posh food, all the stops pulled out for this one event that the university put on for its staff. And I'd been looking forward to it. Simon and I had been together a long time. We were comfortable with each other, I guess you could say. So, I didn't think much of it when we got separated. I knew his colleagues; I didn't need him to hold my hand. I socialized, I danced, I had fun. But I hadn't seen him in a while, which was odd. Usually, I'd spot him across the room and we'd smile and wink and work the room. It was our thing, you know?" I lapsed into silence for a moment, remembering.

Then, taking a deep breath, I continued with my story. "I started to get a bit worried. Had something happened to him? Was he unwell? I'd left my phone in my coat pocket at the check-in kiosk, so I went back to get it, to phone him to see where he was and if he was okay. The coat check-in was unattended, so I opened the door to the closet and found him. Simon. My fiancé."

"With another woman?" Mike asked, leaning

forward, all ears.

I nodded. "With a woman." At first I didn't notice the tears sliding down my cheeks. "A student. And then I knew. I knew why we hadn't set a date for our wedding, how we really hadn't talked about it at all since he'd proposed. Because he didn't want to marry me—I was a front, a cover. And along with the hurt came the anger. The mind-melting overwhelming anger. I couldn't control it, it just... launched out of me. I didn't even have my wand. Magic just flew from my fingertips and changed him into... well, it doesn't matter. The truth of it was, he was human, and I used my magic to harm him."

"I'm so sorry, Harper. That sucks." Mike shook his head.

I sniffed and wiped the tears from my cheeks. "It's okay." I shrugged. "Of course, I was fired from my job pretty much immediately. My boss had been there. Saw the whole thing. Then my witch's license got suspended. I was as low as I thought I could get. So, I came home." I turned to him and placed my hand on his knee, and smiled. "And it was the best thing I've ever done. Being back here in Whitefall Cove made me realize so many things. That I hadn't been truly living in East Dondure. I was simply going through the motions. Yes, I had a job I loved at a big city library. But that was all I had. I didn't have many friends. I didn't have a life."

"But you had a man who loved you. Or at least you thought you did," Mike pointed out.

I was already shaking my head. "That's the thing. I think we both knew that we didn't really love each other. Not the way lovers should. We were friends. I think he proposed to cover up his affair with a student, not because he had an overwhelming desire to marry me. And I accepted for the same reasons. I'd hit thirty —time was running out."

Mike snorted. "That's ridiculous. Thirty is plenty young."

"I know that now. But at the time? God, there's this pressure for a woman about turning thirty. You're meant to have your act together. So, I was ticking boxes. Great job, tick. Fiancé, tick. White picket fence?" I squeezed his knee. "So I get it. When you find someone who makes your heart sing, you just cling on and don't want to let go because deep down you're terrified that this is it, this is your one shot at happiness and even if it doesn't fit right, you try to make it, you try to squeeze and manipulate it, to fit, to work, because otherwise? Otherwise, you're going to be alone."

Mike leaned forward, resting his elbows on his knees, his head hanging low. "That's me and Lexi all right," he admitted. "What I told Jackson was true. It started as a one-night stand. She picked me up. I was flattered. This young, hot woman chose me! And our chemistry? Let's just say we fit together just right. So, when she turned up the next night, and the next, and the next... I didn't turn her away."

"Did you know she was a fox shifter?"

"Oh yeah, could pick it a mile off. And she knew I was a wolf. I thought that was the appeal for her—the taboo. She likes to walk on the wild side; she's daring. All the things I'm not. So, of course, I fell for her. Hard. I thought I could win her over. I thought she was feeling the same way. And today, when she called me and asked me to come to Bean Me Up, that she was tired of all the sneaking around? Oh man, that was music to my ears. I practically ran the entire way, and she met me out the front and kissed me and I felt it all the way to my toes. I've never been happier than I was at that moment."

I didn't tell him I thought her public display of affection had been for our benefit. No need to kick a man when he's down. Instead, I asked, "So what changed? Why did she break up with you hours later?"

He shrugged, flopping back on the sofa again. "I wish I knew. She came around, told me it had been fun, but she was moving on, leaving town. I told her I loved her, begged her not to go, and she laughed in my face and... well, you probably heard the rest." Turning his head, he looked at me. "Don't want to be rude, but what are you doing here, anyway?"

I cleared my throat, glanced at Archie and then

back at Mike. "I actually wanted to talk to you about Lexi. About why you lied about your relationship with her."

"Right." He snorted.

"Yeah. Um. They found a car out at the foxes' compound that they think might be involved in Bruce's shooting."

"And you think Lexi was involved?" He didn't look surprised. Just sad.

I shrugged. "Possibly. I mean, Jackson has his forensic team on it, and I have no idea why Lexi would try to kill Bruce..." I trailed off. I was at a dead end with my investigation. Lexi was leading the way as my number one suspect, but I had no motive for her, only opportunity.

"Maybe it had something to do with when she used to live here?" Mike suggested.

"What do you mean 'used to live here'? Hasn't she always lived here?"

He shook his head. "Nope. She came to town a few months ago. That's why I hooked up with her—a fox —because she was passing through and there'd be no repercussions with the pack. Then she decided to stay awhile. I thought that was because of me."

"But she told you she used to live here? In Whitefall Cove?"

"Yeah. We took a drive one night. And she pointed out this old house, abandoned, run down and boarded up and she pointed to it and said she lived there as a kid. Seemed really sad, too."

"Do you remember where it was?" I tried to tamp down my excitement but failed when my voice came out two octaves higher than normal.

He cocked his head. "You think it's important?"

"It could be."

"Yeah, it was over on Wiltshire. Don't recall the number. Don't think there was one, but it's a faded old weatherboard with wooden boards nailed over the windows and an overgrown front garden. Can't miss it. Neighbors must be thrilled to be living next to such an eyesore."

Standing up, I headed toward the front door. "Thanks so much, Mike, that's really helpful," I said, then stopped and turned back. "You'll be okay?"

He nodded. "I'll be fine. It's not the first time I've had my heart broken. Probably won't be the last. Just feel foolish that I was taken in by a fox. And a young one at that." He'd risen to see me out, and I wrapped my arms around him and hugged him tightly.

"I'm sorry you're hurting," I said.

"Me too," he agreed with a lopsided grin, then stood back, waiting for Archie and me to pass through the door before closing it behind us.

"Right," I said to Archie when we were back in the car. "Wiltshire Drive it is. We have a house to check out."

CHAPTER
NINETEEN

Lexi's childhood home was exactly as Mike had described it. A rundown dump. It looked like it needed to be bulldozed, and I wondered why it hadn't been. Pulling out my phone, I texted Jenna, asking her to dig into who owned the property and when the Sawyers had lived in it. Instead of texting back, she called.

"Do you have a lead?" she asked without preamble.

"I believe I do," I said. "Well, maybe. It depends."

"Harper!"

"I went to see Mike tonight, and he told me that Lexi lived here as a kid. I didn't know Lexi was new to town—or old to town—or whatever."

"From what I know, she turned up a while back. I

don't recall exactly when. Got a job as a barista at Bean Me Up."

"And now lives out at the foxes' compound. Great place for fox drifters," I confirmed.

"I'll see what I can find out. Where are you?"

"I'm at Thirteen Wiltshire Drive," I replied.

"You're there? Harper, it could be dangerous," she warned.

"Jenna, no one's here. It's boarded up. I'm going to have a quick look around the outside and then head back to The Dusty Attic. Archie and I have been working on the crime board this evening and we've made some real progress. Meet me there later if you want."

"I will," Jenna promised. "I've just submitted my copy for tomorrow's story on the car they impounded from the foxes' place. I'll see what I can dig up on the Wiltshire house and I'll meet you at The Dusty Attic in a few."

Disconnecting the call, I opened the door and climbed out of the car, looking at the dark shadow of the house where Lexi Sawyer had grown up as a child. What had happened here that the house was now abandoned?

"You coming?" I asked Archie. He strutted past with his tail in the air as if affronted I'd ask such a question. Using the flashlight on my phone, I followed him down the side of the house and into the back garden. I'd been intending to walk the perimeter of the house, but when I got to the back door and saw that the wood planks that had been nailed over it were now on the ground and the door ajar—well, who could resist? Archie was already inside, and I followed.

The floorboards creaked as I stepped over the threshold and straight into what was once the kitchen. It smelled old and musty, underscored with an earthy scent. I swung my light around and caught sight of Archie as he disappeared through another doorway.

"Archie! Wait!" I didn't know why I was whispering, but I hurried after my cat, regardless. Then I noticed it. On the floor, in the dirt and dust, not just Archie's paw prints, but bigger paw prints. And booted footprints. Someone had been here. "Duh, Harper," I whispered to myself, "obviously someone has been here. That's why the back door is open." Archie darted left, and I hurried after him, into a bathroom. Pausing in the doorway, I couldn't believe my eyes.

"Meow!" Archie announced.

I nodded. "I see it." A potted plant sat in the bathtub. "We have to assume this is the missing borrio bud plant." I moved closer and snapped a photo, then sent it to Jenna with the question: Is this yours?

She texted back immediately.

Yes. Get out of there now.

I didn't need telling twice. Lexi was the murderer.

She'd killed Whitney, had tried to kill Bruce and had already threatened me. And despite my burning curiosity to find out why she'd done those things, self-preservation was high. I was in an abandoned house at night. It was spooky as all hell, and I'd just discovered who the killer was. I knew how horror movies usually ended.

"Let's go," I whispered to Archie, hurrying back down the hallway and out the back door.

Archie was behind me when he made a sound I'd never heard before. A growl. Long, low and deep. Then he launched through the air, hitting me in the back as he used my body to springboard his momentum over my head. I lost my balance and fell, smashing my face into the dirt. Spitting out rubble, I lifted my head to see Archie yowling and growling in front of me, his fur on end, his tail puffed up to twice its size. He spat and swiped his claws out. Another growl joined the mix. Different from Archie's. I rolled to the side to see a fox at the corner of the house. Archie spat again and shuffled forward, his warning clear. He was protecting me. The fox backed up, cast us one last glance, then ran away.

Slowly, Archie's hackles settled and his tail de-floofed. Clambering to my feet and ignoring the stinging in my cheek where I'd face planted, I scooped him up in my arms and kissed his head. "Thank you." Hurrying to the car, I deposited him inside before climbing in after him and locking the doors.

"It had to be Lexi, right?" I asked, my hands only shaking a little bit as I put the key in the ignition and started the car. Archie's meow assured me he agreed. Connecting my phone to the car's Bluetooth system, I called Jackson as I pulled away.

"I think the killer is Lexi Sawyer," I told him as soon as he answered. "She used to live in Whitefall Cove as a kid. At Thirteen Wiltshire Drive. I was just there, and it's abandoned now, but someone had been inside, and when I went in, I found the borrio bud plant stolen from Jenna's greenhouse in the bathtub."

"Where are you now?"

"Heading to The Dusty Attic. I'm meeting Jenna there."

"Good. When you get there, keep the doors locked. Understand?"

"Yes, I understand. But Jackson?" There was something in his voice, something that heightened my sense of danger. "Did you find something else? On Lexi?"

"I'll tell you later," he said gruffly.

"Okay. Is Gran safe? Would Lexi go after her? Because a fox just saw me leave that house. I think it was her."

"Not good," he muttered, which wasn't what I needed to hear. "Is she at home? Alone?" he asked.

"She was on a date when I left. I'll call, see if she's home yet. If not, I'll tell her to stay put."

"If she's home, pick her up and take her with you to The Dusty Attic. I'll meet you there. Do not leave until you've heard from me."

"Okay." I disconnected the call and glanced at Archie. "It's getting real, eh?"

Gran's date had been a bust, and she was already at home, so I swung by to pick her up. "I'm perfectly capable of defending myself," she grumbled, waiting for Archie to move to the back seat so she could ride up front.

"I know you are." I tried to stretch my mouth into a reassuring smile, pretty sure I just ended up baring my teeth at her. "But humor me, okay? Plus, don't you want to know all that we've discovered? Archie and I were updating the crime board, and it all started falling into place."

"Yes, I do, which is why I agreed to let you come get me." Gran was fearless, which I admired greatly because I currently had more than enough fear for the two of us. Lexi Sawyer had killed one person, attempted to kill another, and now knew that *I* knew. She'd be gunning for me for sure. Jackson had better catch her first, or I'd be more than annoyed if she killed me.

We hustled into The Dusty Attic, and I cursed at the frigid temperature. "Seriously!" I practically shouted, locking the door behind us. "I was here literally an hour ago, and I left the thermostat on."

"I'll see to it," Gran offered, ducking into the storeroom and turning the heating back on. A knock at the door made me scream. I spun and peeked behind the blind to see Jenna outside. I let her in. "Quick." I ushered her in and then locked the door again.

"What happened to your face?" she asked, pausing taking off her coat to peer at my throbbing cheek.

I put a hand up, forgetting I'd used my face to break my fall. "I fell. It's nothing, just a scrape." I brushed off her concern. Gran came back out from the storeroom and lit the open fireplace and the warmth of a roaring log fire quickly dispelled not only the chill but also my fear. We were safe. Even if Lexi knew we were here, she couldn't get in. Just to be sure, I double-checked the door. Still locked.

"Jiminy Cricket, but you're making me nervous," Gran protested. "Here." She pointed to the crime board I'd left on display. "Bring us up to speed on this." It was a distraction technique, but it worked. Gran sat in the armchair I'd pulled around for Archie earlier, Jenna perched on one arm, while Archie curled up on Gran's lap. I stood by the board and took them through what we'd discovered.

"Of course, we still need Jackson to confirm it was Lexi in the abandoned house on Wiltshire Drive," I said when I'd finished, "and that it's her prints on the pot plant."

"The chances of it being a different fox shifter are pretty slim," Jenna said, and I nodded in agreement. True.

"I just don't know why," I admitted, tucking my hair behind my ears. "What did Lexi have against the Sims?"

A fist banging against the front door had me swiveling my head so fast I almost gave myself whiplash. "I'll get it," Jenna volunteered, hopping up and crossing the room. She peeked behind the blind, announced, "It's Jackson," and opened the door.

"Everyone okay?" he asked, closing the door behind him. I noticed he didn't lock it and balled my hands into fists, a fierce mental debate going on in my head. If he'd locked it, it would mean Lexi was still on the loose. But he'd left it unlocked, which meant he'd caught her. Right? Noticing my distraction, he reached back and flicked the snib and my heart almost stopped in my chest.

"Oh geez," he muttered, "you've gone as white as a sheet. And what happened to your face?"

"Will people stop asking that?" I pouted. "You're all making me feel like I'm disfigured."

He crossed to me and tilted my face up to the light. "That's a nasty graze," he murmured, his thumb sliding across the skin just beneath my cheekbone. "You should get that looked at."

"Oh, look at you lot," Gran grumbled. "Let me see." She pushed Jackson out of the way and pinched my chin to get a closer look. With a click of her tongue, she whipped out her wand, waved it in front of my face, and the stinging stopped. "That's better." She nodded and resumed her seat. "Harper just brought us up to speed with her investigation," Gran told him. "Now it's your turn. What've you got?"

"She's still on the run, isn't she? She slipped through your net. You locked the door. You wouldn't have locked the door if you'd caught her, which means she's still out there and she knows I know she's a killer." The hysteria rose in my voice, but I couldn't stop it. Jackson caught my hand, drawing my attention to him and not the fact that a madwoman who wanted to kill me was on the loose.

"We got her. You're safe. I locked the door because I could see it was freaking you out that I didn't."

Feeling a little foolish, I allowed myself to enjoy the warmth of his hand for a second longer before disentangling from him and going to sit on the other side of Gran's armchair. "Continue."

"First, thank you, Jenna, for your fast intel on the property at Wiltshire Drive." He smiled at Jenna, who nodded.

"What? What intel? Why didn't you tell me?" I demanded, head swiveling between the two of them.

"I was coming here to do that very thing," Jenna told me, "but when you sent me the photo of the borrio bud, I phoned Jackson to tell him while I was on my way here."

"And just what was this intel?"

"That Lexi's mother owned the property on Wiltshire Drive until four years ago. She was a struggling single mom, and the bank foreclosed and kicked Lexi and her mom out."

"But... did the bank sell the house? Why is it sitting empty?"

"The bank couldn't get an offer that would cover the debt owed. And then Lexi's mom killed herself," Jackson said. I clapped a hand over my mouth. How awful. "Lexi was taken in by her mother's clan in Alabama, but when Lexi turned twenty-one, she came back to Whitefall Cove."

"For revenge," I said.

"She says for justice," Jackson said. "She's spent four years plotting how to kill those responsible for uprooting her life. When she started work at Bean Me Up, Jenna came in one day after she'd been gardening, and she smelled the borrio bud. It goes without saying that foxes have a keen sense of smell."

"But that was months ago," Jenna pointed out. "Why wait all this time?"

"To integrate herself into the community. To become a valued member of society and lessen her chances of being a suspect."

"Smart." Gran nodded.

"A little," Jackson agreed. He directed his next words at me. "Then you came home and forced her hand."

"Forced her hand? What do you mean?"

"Whitney started acting all jittery and weird and Lexi thought she was on to her. So, she rushed it. Initially, she was going to poison both Whitney and Bruce in their home, but she ran out of time, so she took a takeout cup from Bean Me Up, prepared the poison and hid the cup behind the counter until Christina came in and requested the usual order. Christina didn't see Lexi switch the cups."

"But why kill Whitney? Bruce is the bank manager. He's the one who would have foreclosed on the loan," Jenna pointed out.

"Whitney was the realtor who put it on the market. She had all the furniture cleared out and dumped. And Lexi overheard her saying after her mom had killed herself, that the house was an albatross and no one would buy it now thanks to the silly woman who'd offed herself there."

"Wait, so Lexi's mom killed herself at the house?" I asked.

Jackson nodded. "Broke in, cut her wrists in the bath. Whitney discovered the body during a showing."

"How awful," I whispered. Gran patted my knee.

"So... it was Lexi who threw the brick through my window?"

"It was. You were getting too close. The car we impounded? It was used in a corner store robbery in Alabama. And despite it being thoroughly cleaned, we recovered a hair from the driver's headrest. A match to Lexi."

"So, you're saying Lexi robbed a store, drove all the way here, holed up at the foxes' compound and kept the car hidden there while she integrated herself into the community, then killed Whitney?"

"Exactly," Jackson said. "But she didn't have the luxury of time to get rid of Bruce. She rushed it. She used the car she'd kept hidden all this time and shot him. Unfortunately, she didn't kill him. Now everyone was on guard, everyone was suspicious. She was leaving town when we caught her."

"What about Mike?" Jenna asked, but I was already shaking my head.

"She was using him. I'm not even sure why, beyond having a good time. I went to see him tonight, and she was breaking up with him. It wasn't pleasant." I suddenly had a lightbulb moment. "That's why she was at her old house! She was tying up loose ends. Break up with Mike and tell him she's moving on

—that way, it's common knowledge. He'd tell people she'd left. Then go by the old house and take the borrio bud plant, so there'd be no evidence to tie it to her. Only, Archie and I turned up and disturbed her before she could get it."

"You're lucky she ditched the gun she'd used on Bruce." Jackson shook his head.

"What about the rash on Bruce's arm?" Jenna asked. "Was it from the borrio bud?"

Jackson shook his head. "No. Turns out Wendy was right on that. We swabbed his arm and shirt; no traces of the plant. Something else triggered an allergic reaction. Bruce was not involved in the death of his wife."

"Finally!" Whitney's voice behind my left shoulder had me launching off the armrest with a scream. Spinning, I eyeballed the ghost of Whitney Sims hovering a foot off the floor behind the armchair where we'd all been sitting, for Gran and Jenna had joined me in my scramble across the floor. Archie hissed and his hackles rose, along with his spine, in a spectacular arch that was both impressive and intimidating. I made a mental note to make sure I gave him an extra treat when we got home.

"Whitney?" My voice wobbled, and I cleared my throat. "Have you been haunting my store?"

"I've been trying to get your attention," she whined, "but none of you could see me. The only thing that worked was turning that darn thermostat off, but even then, you didn't know I was here."

"Did you know it was Lexi who killed you?" I asked. "And how come we can see you now?"

Whitney pointed at Jackson. "It's him." Then she pointed at me. "And you."

"Us?" We spoke in unison.

"I tried communicating with you. No answer," Jackson accused.

"It's something about her power and your ability," Whitney said. "She's all glowy with magic, like a halo."

I looked at Jackson and mimed she's crazy with my finger at my temple. "I don't have any magic, Whitney," I reminded her. "It's on lockdown."

"It's not," she argued, arms crossed over her chest.

I repeated my original question. "Did you know all along that it was Lexi who killed you?"

Whitney shook her head. "No, I didn't. I was trying to communicate with you to let you know it wasn't Bruce. I knew you'd all think that, but it wasn't him."

"How could you be sure?" Jenna asked.

"Because I knew everything. I knew about him and Wendy. I knew she was pregnant. I knew they were getting ready to make a life together. And," she held up a hand, "despite what you may think, I'd come to terms with it. I'd gotten over all my feelings of jealousy and rage, because what Bruce said to me eighteen months ago when he asked for a divorce? It finally sank in. He said we loved each other but weren't *in love* anymore. And that I needed to live my own life. And so, while I was making my own plans to set up my realtor business—for real—I watched Bruce and Wendy slowly fall in love. Initially, I wanted to hurt them. Both of them. I took control of Bruce's assets, planned to hit him where it hurt the most." She shrugged. "But then you came back to town. An example of what can happen when you allow your emotions to rule. It backfired spectacularly for you and I realized that all the judgment I was heaping on you, well... people would say that about me. I'd rather walk away with my head held high."

"Gee thanks," I muttered. "So the day I came in to sign the papers, did you have the keys all along? Were you messing with me?"

She tossed her hair over her shoulders and glared at me. "I had temporarily misplaced them. It wasn't deliberate."

"Well, you're free to go, Whitney. The mystery of your death is solved. Move into the light or whatever it is spirits do." I waved an arm around, indicating she could leave.

She laughed, smoothed down her dress, and tossed her head again. "Oh no, I'm not going anywhere. I'm here to stay."

I looked at her in horror. "You can't be serious."

"I've thoroughly enjoyed watching your investigation." She floated toward us and it was disconcerting, to say the least. "I've decided to stay. You're looking at Whitefall Cove's very first ghost detective."

Are you ready for book two, **Witch Way to Romance & Ruin***? Get it here:*
www.janehinchey.com/romanceandruin

Thank you for reading! If you enjoyed this book, I'd greatly appreciate your review.

You can find a complete list of my books, including series and reading order on my website at:

www.JaneHinchey.com

Join my newsletter here:

www.JaneHinchey.com/subscribe

And finally, join my readers group on Facebook here:

www.JaneHinchey.com/LittleDevils

Thank you so much for taking a chance and reading my book . It's readers like you who make this journey worthwhile and fuel my passion for storytelling. Your support means the world to me, and I can't wait to share more exciting stories with you in the future.

xoxo
Jane

FREE BOOK OFFER

Want to get an email alert when a new book is released?

Sign up for my newsletter today,

https://janehinchey.com/subscribe

and as a bonus, receive a FREE e-book of

Cupcakes & Curses!

READ MORE BY JANE

Find them all at www.JaneHinchey.com/books

<u>The Ghost Detective Mysteries</u>

#1 Ghost Mortem

#2 Give up the Ghost

#3 The Ghost is Clear

#4 A Ghost of a Chance

#5 Here Ghost Nothing

#6 Who Ghost There?

#7 Wild Ghost Chase

#8 Easy Come, Easy Ghost

#9 Life Ghost On

<u>Witch Way Paranormal Cozy Mystery Series</u>

#1 Witch Way to Magic & Mayhem

#2 Witch Way to Romance & Ruin

#3 Witch Way Down Under

#4 Witch Way to Beauty & the Beach

#5 Witch Way to Death & Destruction

#6 Witch Way to Secrets & Sorcery

The Gravestone Mysteries

#1 Fur the Hex of it

#2 Battle of the Hexes

#3 What the Hex

The Midnight Chronicles

#1 One Minute to Midnight

#2 Two Minutes Past Midnight

#3 Third Strike of Midnight

Clean Scene Inc.

#1 All in Vein

PARANORMAL ROMANCE/URBAN FANTASY

The Awakening Trilogy

Hell's Angel Trilogy

The Enforcer Series (4 books)

Standalones

Returned

Secret Fates

Destiny's Touch

Blood Cursed

Heart of Darkness

ABOUT JANE

Hi there! I'm Jane, crafting tales of paranormal cozy mysteries sprinkled with urban fantasy romance. Between sips of coffee and dodging my mischievous cats, I immerse myself in stories where magic meets everyday life.

Once known as Zahra Stone in the world of steamy urban fantasy, I've now merged those fiery tales under the Jane Hinchey banner. Off the page you'll find me binging on true crime documentaries or sneaking in a Power Nap. Dive into my stories and join me on an enchanting journey!

Find me here: www.janehinchey.com

f facebook.com/janehincheyauthor

⊙ instagram.com/janehincheyauthor

a amazon.com/Jane-Hinchey/e/B0193449MI

BB bookbub.com/authors/jane-hinchey

g goodreads.com/jane_hinchey

Printed in the USA
CPSIA information can be obtained
at www.ICGtesting.com
LVHW091601180924
791239LV00002B/4

9 780994 600790